Cut Loose

Lucy Chesser

Cut Loose

For Erin, Atty & Rex

Cut Loose
ISBN 978 1 74027 509 5
Copyright © text Lucy Chesser 2008
Cover: Atticus Rex

First published 2008
Reprinted 2017

GINNINDERRA PRESS
PO Box 3461 Port Adelaide SA 5015
www.ginninderrapress.com.au

1

Hotel Sugar, Medan, Sumatra, October 2003

Ethan can't quite believe he will be sleeping in this filthy flea-pit of a room. He looks around in utter dismay. Yellow and brown walls – what colour was the paint? It's impossible to tell. Spotted here and there are gross-looking greyish and brown stains, like mucous – or worse. There are dozens of them. The closer he looks the more there seem to be.

The little brown spots at bed height are probably blood – a sure sign of bed bugs, according to Jon. There are grey finger smudges all over the place, though how anyone could bring themselves to touch these walls is beyond him. It's like the room has been home to a dozen men – Ethan can't imagine a girl ever setting foot in here. Bloody hell, is he blind?

"Pretty bad, huh?" says Jon, who has already claimed the better of the two narrow saggy-looking beds. His backpack is tossed on top and he stands stretching his tall body, his long arms almost touching the roof. "But it's only seventeen thousand and it's only for one night."

"That's three bucks – right?" says Ethan.

"Yeah. It's about five thousand rupiah to the dollar, so about three dollars."

"Well, next time, how about we pay six bucks and get something twice as good." Ethan's tone is sarcastic.

Jon's face flushes red. He resists the urge to thump his younger brother.

But Ethan isn't finished paying out: "Dunno how I'm supposed to sleep with this stink. It's the most I can do not to chuck up right now." Angrily Ethan dumps his backpack on the floor.

Jon can see Ethan doesn't want to touch the bed let alone flop down on it, no matter how exhausted he is. Despite himself, he's feeling responsible and guilty for bringing Ethan here. "It's not that bad – you'll get used to it," he says sharply.

He'd like to leave Ethan here and go off wandering on his own, find a bar, meet some travellers. Meet a girl – Christ, he's only nineteen. He should be out there doing nineteen-year-old stuff. But you can't leave a fourteen-year-old in a flea-pit hotel in Medan on his own.

And Jon is getting increasingly pissed off with himself, because more and more he doesn't like the smell in this room either. He'd been so tired and relieved to get out of the hellish traffic that he'd barely poked his nose in the door before taking it. With the front open-air restaurant packed with Western travellers coming and going, he'd been worried they'd miss out on a room altogether.

Standing in here now, with no window to outside and the stifling tropical heat, the problem with the bloody place is obvious. In the corner of the room head-high walls separate the bathroom area from sight. But it has no roof to hold in the odours, and the thick smell of the old piss and shit of strangers is just wafting over the top. That's why Jon's chosen the far bed. The one near the wall with the holes in it that look like peep holes.

"What the fuck is this?" says Ethan. He's swung open the rusty metal door to the bathroom.

Jon comes to stand behind him, looking over his shoulder. Ethan has grown three inches in the last six months, but Jon still towers over him.

"It's a squat toilet," he says assessing the grim little room.

Set flat into the floor is a white ceramic fixture, the centre a shallow bowl, like a squashed toilet, tapering to a dirty-looking water filled hole. Obviously where the waste is meant to end up. Either side are two places for feet to stand, complete with tread to prevent slipping.

"How do you use it?" says Ethan.

"I know as much as you do," says Jon. "I've seen a photo before, but the Indonesian teachers at school didn't go into the finer details."

"How do you flush it?"

"You take that ladle and pour water from that tub. The tub is called a *bak mandi* and it's used for showering too. You stand on the floor, soap up and wash yourself down. That's why the floor is so wet in here."

"Disgusting," mutters Ethan.

Jon doesn't see how, but he lets the comment go. "How about we go get a Coke and some food?"

"I'll meet you out there," says Ethan. "I gotta use this thing. Which way do I face, do you think?"

Ethan is happier when Jon has gone. He unzips his fly and takes a leak, using the ladle to wash down his feet and legs where some of the spray got him. This'll take practice, he thinks. But he's in a slightly better mood already. Having used the toilet and tossed water around, the room is less disgusting to him somehow, and he's already thinking about food.

He had loved the assortment of foods in Malaysia, the Indian food, Chinese and Malaysian food. Georgetown in Penang where they had stayed at the backpackers, was a real buzz, with tandoori ovens on street corners and chickens on long skewers lowered into the giant ceramic drums, right in front of you. It was all lights and action and great smells. Even the rats – the size of cats – had been exciting to him.

And despite his display to Jon, he is excited to be in Indonesia. He'd got a real buzz out of going from one country to another so easily (and so cheaply – about thirty Australian dollars) by ferry. He was amazed at the things that the local people were taking with them. Market foods, boxes of electrical goods, bags of fabric – like they'd gone to a whole other country to do their weekly shopping. And despite feeling sick, he'd found the catamaran ride interesting. They ran music videos and horror movies that were so violent he couldn't believe families were just sitting there watching them. Men with long Samurai swords slicing and dicing each other, blood spurting from severed limbs, and little primary school kids sucking down Coke while they watched it – it was wild. And when he tired of that, the show out the window was pretty good too. The ferry rocketed along on the tops of the waves dashing by all sorts of interesting little boats. They were all so different from the fancy looking yachts he'd seen at St Kilda marina. These things looked like death traps, half sunk, with laundry hanging off makeshift clothes lines. People were living there, right out in the middle of the ocean with not a bit of land in sight. It wasn't hard to imagine the pirates that Jon said still attacked ships sailing these waters.

And he had been looking forward to exploring Sumatra. Just the sound of it was a thousand times more exciting than Malaysia. In Sumatra there were volcanos, impenetrable jungles, tigers, rhinoceroses, orang-utans and there was the danger of a near civil war going on in the north. Jon had assured him they'd stay well away from the trouble, but just the idea of armed rebels sheltering in the jungle excited Ethan beyond what he was prepared to admit to Jon. It could be really cool.

And now he's here he's keen to get stuck into the Indonesian food. He could go a satay chicken now and some nasi goreng – the Indonesian fried rice.

But first he wants to change his T-shirt and have a wash. Medan, though he's only been here an hour or two, seems totally filthy and polluted and he can feel the city's dirt sticking to his sweaty skin. Opening his backpack he takes out his only clean T-shirt. Then, as an afterthought, he grabs his two dirty ones and some soap. In the bathroom he rinses them out under the tap and strings them up on the travel line.

He takes his blue silk sleep sheet from his backpack and lays it out on the bed. At least it will mean he'll not have to touch the mattress. He examines the picture a second. Then he drags the bed frame at least a foot from the wall so there is no possibility he'll accidentally reach out and touch those filthy walls in his sleep. Those stains are totally disgusting. He hates to even think about what they could be.

2

Restoran, Hotel Sugar

Jon is drinking his glass of icy-cold Bintang beer and trying to relax. It isn't easy. There are motorcycles tearing up and down the street just a few metres away, their noisy two-stroke engines rattling in his brain like machine guns. Then there are the street vendors ringing bells and calling out, and every minute or two a truck whirls by with its deep growling engine and squealing, grunting brakes. And of course there is the Bob Marley CD blaring out from the restaurant itself, with Buffalo Soldier competing loudly with the even louder Call to Prayer, for the Muslims broadcast over loudspeakers from the massive mosque just a hundred metres down the road.

He's found himself a seat in this crowded, grotty open-air bar out the front of the hotel. There are about a dozen or so rough bamboo tables, with beer-drinking, smoking Westerners in clunky bamboo armchairs clustered around them. Gathered around them are a number of chain-smoking young Indonesian men, all with long black hair tied back, sunglasses and an attitude to match the Bob Marley CD. They all seem connected to the hotel somehow, but there are dirty plates left lying on many tables, with empty bottles and large ashtrays made out of coconut shells stuffed with ash and butts. No one – not the staff and not the travellers – cares, though. There's no pretending that anyone actually wants to be here. All the travellers are just here on their way to somewhere else. And the Indonesian men hanging about are hoping to go with them as drivers or guides. Tidying up just isn't on the agenda. Ridiculously large over-full backpacks lay about everywhere, just being stepped and tripped over, till their owner's transport arrives and they are dragged out the door, to some waiting minivan double parked out the front.

Jon is annoyed with himself. He has let Ethan get to him, when he knows that is just what he was trying to do all day. He can be a total shit when he tries. First he didn't want to get up early, then he complained about not being able to get McDonalds, then he didn't like waiting for the ferry. Then he was complaining saying he likes Malaysia and why can't they just hang around there for a week, instead of going all the way to Sumatra – in a whole other country – to probably not be able to find someone they'll hate anyway. And then it was all Jon's fault Ethan felt seasick all the way across.

Ethan hasn't come right out and called Jon selfish, but that's what's resting, unspoken, just beneath the surface. And, after a whole day of it, Jon has had enough. Even though he's in Medan – one of the dirtiest and polluted of Indonesia's cities – he's telling himself he's actually excited to finally be in Indonesia. As far as he is concerned, Ethan can just shut up and get out of his head space for a while.

There are about six or seven people Jon doesn't know at the table with him. So far no one has acknowledged he is there, which is fine with him. Three of the people are Indonesian guys, of about his age and they are working on a Western traveller each, trying to set up a tour or a motorbike hire. They are being quite pushy and Jon is interested to watch how the travellers handle it.

There is an earnest-looking German couple where the man seems to get to do all the talking. Jon finds the German way of speaking amusing: "And we will be able to make photo, *ja*?" says the man. He wants a close-up contact with an orang-utan and the two of them have some pretty heavy-looking photographic equipment.

"Ya, ya! No problem!" says his guide. They are striking a deal. It looks like he will be getting a tour bus to Bukit Lawang to the orang-utan viewing centre tomorrow and paying ten times what the local buses would cost. And the guy he's talking to is also an official guide – he keeps flashing his photo ID – and it looks like they'll be doing a jungle trek with him too. There are hundreds of "official guides" – they pay a fee for the privilege but it doesn't mean they know the jungle. But Jon's staying out of it. It's a stupid way to hire a guide, but the poor Sumatran guy is just trying to make a living.

On the other side of the table is a young British backpacker who clearly thinks he's too cool for school with his Indonesian clove cigarettes and his red bandana. But the touts will get nowhere with him because he seems only interested in getting to the north so he can meet the rebels involved in the conflict up there. Or so he says. The Indonesian guy he's talking with seems uncomfortable about the topic and in the end he moves away leaving red-bandana guy on his own. Mr Cool pulls out a serious-looking book and starts to read.

Jon has seen plenty of wankers like him sitting around the groovier coffee shops near home in Northcote. So it's not surprising that he is much more interested in a very attractive girl who is sitting at the same table as him, chatting with another "official guide". The girl is clearly European, but from what country Jon can't tell. Her English is faultless, but there is an occasional very sexy lilt in her otherwise accentless speech. Dutch, Jon guesses. And cute.

He sips his beer and casually scans the menu. He's going to order nasi goreng, but doesn't want to get up and maybe lose his seat. This place is kind of chaotic; the Indonesian guy talking to the girl is sitting on the table.

Jon wonders whether she has noticed him yet. She has shoulder-length brownish blonde hair and gorgeous strong-looking shoulders, like a swimmer.

He knows some girls find him attractive, but he is aware he is unusual-looking and he's always worried how girls will respond. Even though he has inherited some of his father's straight black hair and brown eyes and skin, he tells himself he is obviously not going to be mistaken for a local. He has his Australian grandfather's height, footballer's shoulders and he stands head and shoulders over most Indonesian men. And he has his mother's high cheekbones and her thin, pointed European nose. Though he's a fairly modest kind of bloke, he's secretly always thought his Western facial features looked pretty cool along side his vaguely Asian eyes and colouring.

The girl seems to be tiring of the discussion with the hopeful guide over her itinerary. "Thank you, but I want to take the local bus," she says for about the fifteenth time.

She's doing well to keep her tone polite, Jon thinks. He likes that. He reaches out and taps the young guy on the shoulder. Pointing to his empty glass, he says, "*Satu lagi*. One more."

"You want one too," the Indonesian guy asks the girl.

"Sure, why not," she says smiling.

Jon notices her teeth. They are straight and white and she has a small dimple in one cheek, because her smile is slightly lopsided.

"I'm Jon," he says as an opener.

"Katrin," she says, but what she says next is drowned out as a large truck grinds past the front, engine roaring, belching foul exhaust everywhere.

"Nice place," Jon says mildly, as soon as the racket dies down. The exhaust is stinging his eyes, and he can't believe people are actually choosing to smoke cigarettes on top of the pollution. But he's struck the right note and he is pleased when Katrin laughs. A good start. "Where are you from?" he asks.

"Belgium," she says. "And you – you must be Australian."

"Is the accent that strong?"

The Indonesian guy is back with the beer, which is poured into glasses that have come straight from the freezer and are coated in ice. Katrin introduces him as Hamid. He squats down and starts to work his spiel on Jon. He says he is a guide from Bukit Lawang and he can arrange cheap transport there so Jon can see the orang-utans and then he can take him on a trek through the jungle.

"*Terima kasih, Hamid. Tetapi saya mau naik kendaraan umum ke Bukit Lawang. Mungkin saya akan bertemu Anda di Bukit Lawang, dan mungkin saya akan pergi ke hutan dengan Anda.*"

Jon is pleased to see the understanding in Hamid's eyes.

"*Bisa bahasa Indonesia!*" he says. "You speak Indonesian!"

"What did you say?" asked Katrin.

"I just said I wanted to get public transport, but that maybe I'd see him at Bukit Lawang and maybe I'd do a trek with him."

"I saw you arrive," says Katrin. You have a friend with you?"

"Yeah, my brother."

"He seems very young. Are your parents with you?"

"No. Ethan is fourteen. I'm his guardian." Jon doesn't really know what to say next. It all seems kind of serious and personal for a first chat. "We're on holidays," he adds.

Katrin doesn't pry. Instead she asks the usual traveller's questions. Where have you been, where are you going next? Jon explains that he is on uni holidays and has about three months in total. They've spent a week in Malaysia and now intend to spend about a month in Sumatra. Maybe longer. After that, he's not sure. Maybe Java and Bali, or maybe Thailand and Laos. They haven't decided yet.

In the middle of all of this, Jon manages to order his nasi goreng. Katrin orders a hamburger and chips – she is sick to death of Indonesian food – "rice and noodles, noodles and rice". It turns out she'd deferred university to be wildly irresponsible and travel through south-east Asia for six months. She flew into Bali five weeks ago and has made her way overland through Bali and Java. For the last three days she's been on a bus ride from hell, coming all the way from Jakarta to Medan.

"So you're off to Malaysia?" Jon says, hiding his disappointment.

She pulls the hamburger apart. The chips look good, but the bread looks like a couple of undercooked sponges. "Not yet. I've three weeks left on my visa and I hope to spend that time here. I've friends coming this way and I expect to see them any day now."

"You'll wait here for them?"

"God no! One day is enough. Tomorrow I'll go to Bukit Lawang for a few days. My friends will head straight there anyway and I'm sure there will be email there. It's very touristic, I hear."

Touristic. That's that very cute European accent seeping through again. Jon likes it.

"We're going there too," he says. Should he suggest they go together? Of course not – that would be too pushy. Clearly uncool.

"You prefer to go by tourist bus?" asks Katrin.

"No. Local, provided it isn't too ridiculously difficult."

"Where is your brother?" Katrin asks changing the topic.

Jon wonders how many beers she's had. There are heaps of empties on the table, but she doesn't appear drunk.

"Dunno. In our room, I guess. Maybe he's fallen asleep."

"Maybe you two want to travel with me tomorrow? On the local bus."

Just as she says that, Jon spots Ethan standing at the bar. He's talking to red-bandana man and as he looks Ethan raises a glass of beer to his lips.

Quickly Jon drops his eyes back to Katrin, who is picking at her last remaining chips. "Sure," he says. "We were going to leave about seven-thirty tomorrow morning. That OK with you?"

3

Travelling

Ethan is having a ball. He's hanging out the back of a crowded bemo, as it rips through this crazy Medan traffic, his hair blowing wildly about, his eyes streaming. All around him there is noise and motion and pungent ever-changing smells: exhaust, animals, food, sewers. There's trucks and buses and millions of motorbikes busting his eardrums, and horns blaring from everywhere.

The driver of his bemo seems to have a particular problem with *becaks*, the three-wheeled bicycle rickshaws, which keep pulling out blindly into the traffic, their skinny drivers pedalling steadily with their strong sun-browned legs. Ethan stands – with others who don't fit inside – on the backboard holding onto a bar, put there for customers. The speed and movement is exciting. Each time the bemo swerves or brakes suddenly, Ethan absorbs the movement in his legs, like riding a surfboard. It is totally cool and there's an enormous smile on his face.

Jon and Katrin are inside, sitting together on one of the two bench seats running longways down the inside of the van. From what Ethan can see its packed solid in there, with their backpacks, about ten people and a whole bunch of baskets of vegetables. It's a strange kind of public transport, he thinks. Like a ute with a roof and bench seats, all open to the air.

There's about three others hanging on with him, although they keep changing all the time as people jump in and out and off and on. Mainly they're young guys, his age or a bit older. Ethan has a huge smile on his face and everyone is trying to talk to him, lots of "how are you?"s without the English to go further and "*Mau ke mana?*"s, Where are you going?"s which Ethan understands – what a buzz – and can answer, "Bukit Lawang."

Before too long they're out of the city and the bemo is speeding down a narrow bitumen road in what looks like a suburb. The rough, dirty little shop fronts are gone and now there are some open fields, a cow, some rice planted in narrow lots between houses. Still there are motorbikes, but their bemo is bigger and it hugs the centre of the road, the motorbikes swerving out onto the dirt shoulders to get around.

Ethan has felt overwhelmed by the obvious poverty he's seen everywhere around him. Families of five – mum, dad and three kids perched on a motor scooter. Becak men hauling huge loads to and from market for the equivalent of fifty cents. Men and women pulling heavy wooden wagons piled high with scrap metal or broken-up cardboard boxes. Youths with bored expressions squatting in shady doorways, smoking those endless cigarettes.

But now, here and there are some large new houses that look very expensive. Mostly they're painted white, many are two-storey with huge tiled verandas out the front. Invariably they are surrounded by serious concrete walls topped with barbed wire or spikes or, sometimes, broken glass cemented into the wall. It's a bit freaky. Ethan's thinking he'd be scared sleeping in one of these mansions at night, with it so obvious to Medan's millions of poor that you have so much more than they do.

Inside the bemo, Jon is practising his Indonesian on some local women who are returning from the market. They've bought enough vegetables to stock a shop and one of them has two chickens in a cane basket, their little brown heads poking out.

Even though its only two years since Jon did Year 12 Indonesian, he's very rusty and is constantly having to ask the women to repeat themselves. They seem to understand him perfectly, though, but often what he says makes them burst into laughter. He knows what he has learned at school is much more formal than what people actually speak, but he wonders just what he sounds like. Like some Little Lord Fauntleroy with a plum in his mouth and a spike up his bum, no doubt.

He's glad Ethan's been hanging off the back of the bemo. Things were tense between them again this morning. But now he can hear him trying to chat in Indo with people and there's been a stack of laughter out there. Every now and again he's caught a glimpse of Ethan's face and huge grin. He's enjoying himself, Jon thinks, with an enormous feeling of relief that snuffs out the worst of the guilt. OK, so maybe he shouldn't be letting his fourteen-year-old brother race around the streets hanging off the back of a bus without a helmet in a country with a shocking record on road safety and low standards of medical care, but two hundred and sixty million Indonesians live like this all the time. It's a great experience for him. Much better than being left in foster care at home.

And of course he and Katrin are only a few years older than him and here they are, taking the same risks.

Which, of course, was Ethan's argument last night when Jon had challenged him about ordering a beer. "You're drinking," he'd said.

"So."

"So you shouldn't be. Not at fourteen."

"Oh, come on, Jon. You're my brother not my mother. And you drink. You're only a little bit older than me."

"I don't drink much. And the legal age to drink is eighteen."

"No one cares here."

"I care."

"But I don't see why. You'd have had a beer when you were fourteen if you could get away with it. Everyone does it."

Jon gave up then. It was no use arguing. How could it help to tell Ethan that he could have drunk alcohol or done drugs all he liked at fourteen because their mother never laid down rules about anything? But criticising Sharon never got you anywhere with Ethan. He'd just say, "Well, if Mum didn't mind, what do you care?"

The bemo pulls into a bus station and they climb out, leaning their backpacks against a bench. Katrin goes up front and pays the driver. Almost immediately Indonesians start to gather around them.

"Want transport?" says one middle-aged guy.

"Minibus," says another.

"Cigarette," says a man with only one arm, his only hand thrusting an open carton right under Ethan's nose.

Suddenly there are at least eight people there. Ethan can see Jon is caught up with a water-seller and he's started to bargain. This means they're in a buying mood and the other sellers take encouragement from this. A woman has hold of Ethan's hand and she's trying to put a warm bottle of Coke in his fingers. He's trying not to accept it from her and is gently pushing it away. But it's a test of nerve: he's worried it's going to fall and shatter on the concrete, the woman senses he'll grab it if she lets go. So now suddenly it's his and he's trying to pass it back to her saying, "No thanks, I don't want it", then in Indonesian "*Saya tidak mau*", but he knows she's never going to take it back.

Cigarette man has seen what's happened and he's deftly managed to take a pack from the carton with his one hand and he's tucked the rest of the carton under the armpit where the stump is. And now he's trying to pass the cigarettes to Ethan's free hand.

"So these buses to Bukit Lawang leave every thirty minutes," Katrin says. "Do you want to wait here while I go find out which one?" She has returned from the bemo and seems not to notice the sellers.

"Do you want me to do it?" Jon says. He's bought his water and is drinking greedily.

"It's OK. I've learned enough Bahasa to get by. *Saya mau ke Bukit Lawang*. And pointing at the clock for times. It's got me all the way from Bali."

"I'll come too," says Ethan, turning sideways to cigarette man and nestling closer to Katrin. "I want to see you do it. Jon can you pay this lady for my Coke?"

"She'll want the bottle back – they get a large deposit for them," says Katrin.

"I'll tell her we're not going anywhere." Jon replies. "Do you want ice, Ethan? She'll put it in a glass with ice for you, or in a plastic bag."

"A glass. I'll have it when we get the ticket," says Ethan.

Two hours later it's happening again. As the bus rolls in, there are at least fifteen to twenty guys up at the windows, flashing pictures of guest houses and tatty old photos of treks they have supposedly run. There's a hell of a lot of noise and Ethan feels frightened of the desperation he sees in the faces of the young men. Twenty of them wanting business and only three customers. There are no other tourists on the bus. A couple of boys got on about ten minutes ago trying to sell tours and accommodation, and, although they haven't yet given up, Katrin has discouraged them. Ethan is already feeling hassled and he's glad that Katrin and Jon have got a plan worked out.

They'd read the guide book carefully. Bukit Lawang is a tourist town along the banks of the Bohorok River. The road from Bohorok, the local village, stops completely at the southern end of Bukit Lawang township. From there, the tourist settlement is connected only by walking paths, with the Gunung Leuser National Park running along most of the western bank of the river, and hotels and guest houses mainly on the eastern bank. Katrin's plan was to get a room in a guest house near the canoe crossing, right at the northern end of the settlement.

"OK, let's go," says Katrin.

She has her backpack and is down the aisle of the bus before Ethan can think. But he's quicker than Jon, whose large body doesn't fit well into these little Indonesian buses.

Outside, Katrin is speaking to a group of sellers "Where is the permit office?"

"Sorry, miss, permit office closed," says one man.

"Yes, closed," says another.

Ethan hears "closed" muttered by one or two others.

"It's not closed. We know it's not closed," Katrin says, her voice steady.

Katrin had warned Ethan and Jon about this scam. They tell you the office is closed to try to get you into a guest house. There's no real harm in it. But still no one likes to be conned.

"Sorry, miss," says the first guy. "Closed today. You come to my guest house. Have shower, food. Tomorrow get permit."

Several young men are saying similar things.

Katrin is taking care not to make eye contact or focus on any one of them in particular. "No we're staying at Jungle Inn," says Katrin. She says it several times. That's part of the plan. Know where you are going and don't hesitate.

Jungle Inn gets a good write up in the guide books. It's on the eastern bank, right at the far end of the settlement, just beside the national park. It's a perfect location, but also they'll have to walk past just about every other guest house to get there and, if they see something they like, they will stop and check it out.

Ethan waits on the top step of the bus, not wanting to lose his height advantage. The plan was to start walking. The maps show the permit office just next to where the bus stops. As soon as Katrin moves off, he jumps down and is right there beside her. He senses Jon walking behind him.

They've pulled up into a small square, with a few souvenir shops. The road seems to end right here, just like on the map. And there's the permit office. Like clockwork.

When they come out twenty minutes later, with permits in hand, the welcoming committee has gone. With a quick glance at the guide book map, they set off single file down the track on the eastern side of the river. The sky is a deep grey colour and the ground is muddy. It feels like more rain is on the way.

4

Jon's trying not to be too hard on himself. He knows he's placating Ethan by agreeing to take this room, but he figures both of them could do with something clean and special after that filthy hole they slept in last night. This is really nice. It's not the Jungle Inn (which was full) but it's right next door, on the river.

Their room is upstairs with a balcony and a bamboo table and chair to sit at and look at the river. The room has two beds – it has a huge four-poster bed with a mozzie net and a smaller single bed, which he will insist Ethan takes. There's a bathroom, but it's in a totally separate room. It's clean and bright because the bathing part (which has a shower with hot water) has no roof and is completely open to the sky – presumably because people don't mind a little extra water when they're showering. It's pretty cool. There's also a Western toilet with toilet paper. And, as Ethan pointed out, it's only twelve dollars a night.

Katrin has taken a downstairs room. Her room costs about three dollars a night. It has a double-bed-size mattress on the floor, which takes up all the floor space in the room – wall to wall – except for about thirty centimetres between the foot of the mattress and the wall where the door is. She's put her pack there. There is no mozzie net, but Katrin isn't worried. She has her own and at this moment she is standing precariously on a plastic stool on the mattress trying to wind the corkscrew of her Swiss army knife into a crack in the beam above the bed. She'll hang the net off that.

There's a shared bathroom and it is a little grim, mainly because it has no window and nowhere to hang your clothes or towel while you wash yourself. Katrin still isn't entirely used to taking a bath so close to what is effectively a public toilet – practically standing over it. Probably she'll bathe in the river. Or in the presidential suite upstairs. The boys aren't going to mind.

Interesting pair. Jon seems nice, but very serious. And from what she's seen, Ethan is pretty adventurous for a fourteen-year-old. She's seen parents travelling with kids, but not a brother taking his fourteen-year-old brother backpacking. The parents must be pretty permissive.

And then it hits her. Or they don't have parents. Jon had said he was Ethan's "guardian". She hadn't understood. At first she'd smiled thinking it was a joke – as in he was Ethan's "guardian angel". But she disguised the smile when she saw the lack of humour in Jon's eyes. And then he'd changed the topic. Or had she? She didn't remember. After three days sitting on a bus, two beers had wiped her out. She'd been exhausted last night and had gone to bed soon after agreeing to travel with Jon and Ethan.

She's feeling great now, though. And she likes her room. She's going to ask Ethan or Jon to photograph her in it later. A few months ago, she might have found it a little grubby. But it's a lot better than many places she's stayed at. There's quite a lot of mould on the mattress and top sheet, but that's hard for a hotel to avoid, especially in a room like this, whose front door is only about three metres from the river. It's so close that standing just outside the door you can feel a fine mist of water spraying from its fast flowing waters. Katrin's going to enjoy lying in bed listening to the sound of the river roaring past her feet. And possibly a thunderstorm too; the clouds are thick and black and there is definitely rain in the already damp humid air.

The net is up now and she stretches out the corners and tucks them neatly under the mattress. A mozzie-free space to retreat to. She thinks she's going to need it. With this unbelievable damp, the place must be infested and Sumatra has malaria and dengue fever, neither of which she wants to catch.

She steps outside her door and locks it, pocketing the key. This place has a reputation for theft – not that she's left anything of value in the room. Her miniature digital camera is in her shirt pocket in a waterproof bag and her passport, credit card and travellers cheques are in a pouch under her clothes.

She has ten or fifteen minutes to kill. They are all meeting to cross the river at two-thirty p.m. because the orang-utan feeding session is at three. Walking along the river a little, she sits down at a chair and table overlooking the river. It is about ten to fifteen meters wide, brown and moving extremely quickly, swirling around half submerged boulders. There is a bend in the river here and a spot where people obviously get in to swim or wash clothes, but the river seems to be going too fast at the moment to do either of those things.

Across on the other side is a small clearing around some rocks, then behind them the jungle begins, with its millions of intertwined plants densely covering the tall hillside that rises steeply, blocking out the afternoon sun, until it meets the clouds. It's her first glimpse of Sumatran jungle.

And there's an orang-utan standing right there, just across the river.

She can't believe it. She hadn't noticed it. Then it moves, standing up on is legs. It is much smaller than she expects, but she is mesmerised by its long hairy arms and legs and the unbelievable rusty-red colour of its fur. It's like a child, she thinks. Then it looks at her. It is a gaze that is completely without fear. In a moment it has gone, disappearing into the jungle in a blur of red.

A large rain drop strikes Katrin's face with a thud, rolling down her cheek, like a tear drop. She wipes it away. Others follow in quick succession, thudding down as the skies open up with the inevitable downfall.

Within twenty seconds the stream of rain is so thick in the air Katrin can barely see across the river. The roar of it is immense and the ground is awash with water.

Katrin retreats to shelter – the awning of the Jungle Inn's restaurant. It takes only seconds, but she is drenched to the skin. Then she runs back to her room, her feet splashing muddy water onto her bare legs as she goes. Gasping, with water pouring from her hair and shirt, she unlocks her room and, leaning only her arm in, retrieves her rain coat. Still, she thinks, what's the point? I'm already wet. But maybe she'll get cold. Then, scurrying from cover to cover, she makes her way to where the canoe leaves from.

Ethan and Jon are nowhere to be seen, but there are four other travellers there and two Indonesians. All are sheltering from the rain.

"Is the viewing still on? Even with this rain?" she asks one of the Indonesians.

"Yes, yes. Orang-utan still will want food. But maybe it is better you go tomorrow morning."

"Will the rain have stopped?"

"Maybe. Maybe not. It is rainy season. It rains a lot here." He shrugs and heads out into the rain to launch the canoe.

"You look funny." It's Ethan.

"You too," she says taking in his drowned-kitten appearance. Like a kitten he looks much smaller when he's wet, she thinks. She gives him a smile. "Where's Jon?"

"Taking a shower."

For a second she thinks he's serious. Then, Jon comes barrelling out of the rainstorm, swearing his head off, his clothes plastered to his skin and she gets the joke. He's quick, is Ethan.

It takes about ten minutes to get everyone across. The Indonesians organise the canoe; two at a time the travellers sit in the dug-out. It has a rope at each end and someone on the other side pulls it across, while another guy keeps the rope taut. The current is so fast that paddling would have been useless.

Two other travellers go first and Ethan is impatient waiting his turn. But soon enough he's out in the middle of the river, being buffeted about and sprayed with water. Then in a flash he sees a log, spearing down the river right at them. They are right in line to be smashed, but all of a sudden one rope goes slack and the canoe spins right around, so that its nose points downstream instead of across the river. The momentum is extreme and Ethan is thrown onto his back, his hands gripping wildly at the sides of the canoe to prevent being hurled into the river. Out of the corner of his eye, he sees the log sweep by missing them by a metre or so. And then it's over and they are left like fish on a line waiting to be hauled in.

Ethan lets out a holler of excitement and kicks his foot playfully at Jon, who looks like he's suddenly got chalk for blood. "I wish we had a video camera," he says. "Did you see that? That was awesome."

The guy holding the rope needs some help hauling them in, but soon they are on the opposite bank, being helped out of the canoe.

Ethan waves to Katrin on the other side. "Did you see that!" he cries, but the roar of the river is so loud that he can't hear her response.

A couple of Indonesian guys hold the canoe steady, while one gathers in the rope that the quick-thinking fellow on the other bank had dropped. When he has it all together, he throws the end back to the other side and the canoe is pulled back.

Soon they are all across and the ranger is there waiting in his short-sleeved brown uniform. His English is very clear and he gives them a brief introduction to the work at the viewing centre, before setting off, warning them to keep together.

After the crossing, everyone is completely wet, but Ethan doesn't think anyone cares any more. It isn't cold and their effort as they climb up the trail keeps them warm. The rain is almost refreshing.

But the path is slippery and muddy. Ethan is wearing his reef sandals, but they keep getting stuck in the mud, making ridiculous sucking noises as he pulls them out. He's already fallen when he couldn't get his foot clear of the mud quick enough. There are a lot of steps, which is good, because they aren't as slippery, but they're big steps and hard work to climb. The muscles in his quads are burning and when he stops for a rest, his legs tremble like he's just been doing sets of squats at the gym.

Ahead of him Katrin is climbing steadily and apparently with little effort. Ethan gets a very good look at the backs of her legs as she does this. No wonder Jon is keen, he thinks – she's gorgeous. Long legs with beautifully defined calf muscles – like an athlete. But he thinks Jon's going to be disappointed. These friends she's waiting for – he gets the feeling one of them may be more of a friend than the others. There's this guy called Martin, who she met in Bali. She's mentioned him a few times.

They reach a flat section of the trail and the ranger motions for them to be quiet. There is a wooden platform built between three enormous tall trees. It's just three beams, secured to the tree with rough wooden planks nailed over the top.

"Please wait here. Don't try to touch the orang-utan. Although mainly friendly, some have attacked tourists before." The ranger holds up a large plastic bucket. "In this there is a mixture of milk and bananas. We feed them this twice a day. We hope they will become bored with this food and go into the jungle to find better things to eat. When we don't see them here, we have succeeded. The orang-utan here have been rescued. Mainly from private owners. They take them when they are cute babies, but then can't cope with them when they are fully grown. Orang-utan much stronger than person. Now I go to the platform. Soon orang-utan should come. Watch the trees. They are always in the trees."

Ethan finds a log to sit on. It doesn't matter that it's soaked – so is he. He watches as the ranger climbs up onto the platform.

Soon there is a gigantic rattle in the trees and an orang-utan climbs down one of the trees directly onto the platform. It's a mother and Ethan can see her baby clinging to her stomach, its little feet and hands holding on tightly around her middle.

The mother goes straight to the ranger and he hands her a cup of milk. She drinks this like an ordinary person would, then takes a banana and munches on that, washing it down with milk. Baby comes off her stomach and although it stays close, the ranger is able to hand it a banana.

The trees behind them are rustling wildly. Looking up Ethan spots an orang-utan overhead. Soon it too has shimmied down one of the trees and is having its dinner. A fourth joins them. The rangers are totally saturated and the orang-utans don't seem to like the rain either. Ethan is astonished to see one snap off a large leaf, the size of a dinner plate, and hold it by its stem above her head, like an umbrella. She sits there on the platform holding her umbrella in one hand and her cup of milk in the other.

Ethan feels like he could watch this for hours, but after a while he is starting to feel cold and when the ranger climbs back down and motions for them to head off, he is ready.

It's now evening and Jon is going to thank Ethan for insisting they take the room with the hot-water showers. By the time they arrived back at the river crossing, Jon was covered in mud from sliding down the path on his arse. Not very graceful, but then everyone was in the same boat. Katrin was filthy and Ethan was mud from head to toe. At the canoe crossing, he'd wanted to swim the river. He hadn't liked being in the canoe, especially after seeing that floating tree nearly kill them both. Christ, it was close. In the canoe he'd felt trapped, a sitting target. But the Indonesian guy was very firm when he suggested swimming. It was too dangerous at the moment. Maybe tomorrow if the rain stopped, swimming would be OK.

Jon's standing naked under the open-air shower in their room. He's enjoying the sensation of the hot water running down his body warming it while the much colder thicker rain drops slap and tickle his skin. It is kind of excruciating – the contrast: light and shade, heat and cold, pleasure and pain. He's using soap to slide away the mud and the sweat from the long day and he's enjoying that feeling as his skin becomes smooth and slippery. He can't look directly up, because the downpour immediately fills his eyes, but he can see the sky over head is black and menacing.

Power went out about ten minutes ago, so the hot water probably won't last long. Katrin, who had first shower, has lit candles and put three of them around the room – out of the rain, obviously – and it's a nice girl touch that Jon really appreciates. He thinks he looks good in candlelight. It shows up the contours of his body and gives his skin a deep reddish brown colour. The sun has started to brown his skin at his T-shirt line and he admires the way his arms look, muscular and brown. All of a sudden he has an image of swimming tomorrow. The sun has come out and Katrin is watching him. He sees himself through her eyes, dappled light filtering through the rainforest canopy, his shirt off, exposing his slim, muscular chest. He looks good, but he doesn't notice her watching. He is unselfconscious, natural, masculine. Like a movie, his vision cuts to a shot of Katrin emerging from the river in a bathing suit, the fabric clinging to her body.

"What the fuck are you doing in there!" says Ethan. He's unceremoniously swung open the door and is standing there, arms crossed, a picture of annoyance.

"Fuck off!" Jon snaps back, with more venom than he'd intended. He turns his back on Ethan and instantly he feels like crying. He doesn't know why, but the urge is powerful and he chokes back the knot in his throat.

"Well, hurry up, mate," says Ethan. "You'll run the hot water out."

Jon feels like crap. That's Ethan's voice when he's hurt and upset, but he'd rather die than let you know it. Ethan's throaty, big man's voice.

As the door closes quietly, Jon crushes the soap in his fist. Why did he have to swear at him? There's an instant tightness in his scalp and temples; the beginning of a headache. He puts his face is his hands and rubs it fiercely, but the urge to cry is still only barely under control. When Mum had finally died, the choice had seemed simple. Either he applies for guardianship, or Ethan goes into foster care. He'd practically run the house for years anyway, so what difference could it make? He was a responsible person, with a good part-time work history. A law student. They'd get the pension and there was just enough money left over from Nana's will to help out with a few little extra things – like a couple of cheap plane tickets to Asia this summer. Jon knew they'd have to be careful with money, but obviously he'd do better budgeting than Sharon ever had. And Jon really didn't want Ethan in foster care.

But he's always felt strong and capable before – maybe because it was obvious he was doing so much better than his mum even though he was just a kid himself. But now he's a man and Ethan's a kid and he really is responsible for everything.

Guilt and responsibility, like a cancer growing in his gut, seems to run through everything he does these days.

5

The Jungle Inn, Bukit Lawang

When Jon arrives in the restaurant, Katrin is drinking tea and playing chess with the Indonesian guide Hamid, from Medan. It's a huge, airy, barn-like place, with a thatched roof over enormous beams cut from tree trunks. There are tables and chairs for a sizeable crowd – forty or fifty people – but Katrin is the only traveller there.

The whole of Bukit Lawang has this feeling – it's all geared up for the tourist explosion – but where are the tourists? Maybe it's this God-awful weather, thinks Jon.

The game is nearly over and Hamid is in command.

"Shit, shit, shit!" says Katrin as she realises she is about to lose a piece – either her knight or bishop. She can choose which one, but there's nothing she can do to prevent the coming carnage.

Jon goes to the counter. There's no one there so he goes round the door and into the kitchen. The place is quiet. No one is working. There's no food preparation – just a guy lying in a hammock smoking a cigarette. Jon grabs a Coke and a menu.

Back at the table Katrin has sacrificed her knight, but she's already in deep trouble again. The speed with which Hamid moves is extraordinary. Katrin takes time to ponder, but Jon can see Hamid has already calculated all her possible moves and his best countermoves for each. No sooner has her piece touched down on the board, than he's moved again and she's under new pressure. The game is over in minutes.

"You're very good," Katrin says, offering her hand.

"Not so good for a Batak man. We are very good chess players. It's been part of our culture for centuries."

"I'll play you," says Jon.

Katrin picks up the menu. "Shall we order, or wait for Ethan?" she asks.

"Order. He's just got in the shower. I'm starving."

"I'll get someone," says Hamid.

"No, it's OK. I'll go up," she says. "What do you want, Jon?"

"Vegie curry with tofu. Tell them I want it *pedas*."

"What's that?"

Hamid laughs. "Spicy! You like spicy food! Just like Indonesian person."

Katrin walks off to place the order.

"*Ayah saya orang Batak*," says Jon. He surprises himself, but then the Indonesian statement that his father is a Batak man has been rattling around in his head since he boarded the ferry to Sumatra.

Hamid looks surprised. He squints at Jon as if taking a closer look. "*Ayah Anda berasal dari mana?*"

Jon understands, but his Indonesian fails him and he answers in English. "I'm not sure where he's from, exactly. My mother met him at Lake Toba, but I'm not sure if that was where he was from originally."

Hamid is setting up the chessboard. "You looking for him?" he asks.

"Yeah. But it's not a big deal." Jon keeps his tone casual and relaxed. "I haven't seen him since I was a little kid. He's probably dead or has a new family by now. I just wanted to see where he was from."

"What's his name? Maybe I know him?"

Jon hesitates. He doesn't want to say. If he's dead he doesn't want to hear it. Not just now. And if he's alive he doesn't want the grapevine broadcasting to his father that his long-lost son is in Sumatra looking for him. Hamid will understand. "How about I buy you a Coke, instead," he says.

After two quick games of chess Jon is starting to think that Katrin may not have been a bad player after all. Hamid is way too good for him and when their food arrives it seems like a good time to put the board away.

Katrin is very interested to hear that Jon's father is Sumatran. Several times during the game Hamid had made reference to Jon's Batak ancestry, being nice – "Good move. I can see you're a Batak man!" And not nice – "I don't think it's possible your father is a Batak" – when he did something particularly brainless.

Now, as they eat their food, Katrin gently quizzes Jon.

"My father left the family when I was five. But I have fond memories of him."

"And Ethan?"

"Same mother, but his father was a different bloke. That one was gone by the time Ethan was born. I don't even remember him."

"Your mother raised you alone?"

"She tried, I guess. She always had a lot of problems, alcohol, drugs. Then cancer on top of that."

Katrin nods.

Jon shrugs and smiles, as if to say, "That's a long time ago."

But it's not. Not really. Just eight months. And Jon kind of does want to talk about it. But then he doesn't want to come off sounding like a real sad case. If he told the truth, Sharon had been a hopeless drunk, pretty much all the years Jon could remember.

Jon sees his mother spread-eagled on the couch, unconscious. Her arm is outstretched, hanging uncomfortably over the edge, where her fingers have released the lit cigarette which is now burning a smouldering hole in the lino. Jon is seven and he has just come home from school. He goes to the kitchen and fills a saucepan with water and puts out the fire. Then he gathers up two-year-old Ethan from his cot – how long has he been there? He's filthy and hungry, but twenty minutes later he's playing happily with Jon's Matchbox cars, and eating a biscuit.

That had been the worst time. They went into foster care for a while after that. Sharon always claimed it was just a few days, but in Jon's memory it was weeks and weeks. Maybe it just seemed like a long time because it was scary, being moved away from his mum, having to live with people he didn't know. After that, Sharon had a horror of another visit from "Fucking Social Services". She made sure that Ethan and Jon always had proper clothes and lunch money The house was kept clean. "They're not getting any excuse from me," she'd sometimes mutter as she bashed cushions or picked up toys scattered about. Talk like that used to scare Jon half crazy.

During the day, the cask of wine was kept tucked away on top of the fridge. It was only after dinner that it moved down to the coffee table. There she'd sit, in front of the television, drinking herself stupid.

Jon found lots of excuses not to hang around. Playstation. A second TV in his room. Homework. She was always still at it when he called "Goodnight" from his doorway and turned out the light. Some mornings she was still there, passed out, when he got up.

Jon knew this wasn't a great way to live. He'd watched enough TV and read enough books to know what parents were meant to be like. But they were managing OK. Jon and Ethan went to school. There was enough to eat. After Nana died, there was even a bit of money for some luxuries – a new computer, internet, skateboards.

And then the cancer came.

But Jon wants Katrin to fancy him, not feel sorry for him. And he has no need for sympathy. He is doing fine – better than many from much more normal backgrounds.

So he changes the topic, asking her about her friends. There are three of them, a boy-girl couple and a single guy. He heard her telling Ethan about them this morning on the bus, but now he asks more. The couple are Paula (who is English) and Jean, who is French. The single man is Martin and he is French too.

At first Jon was worried about this Martin character. But now he doesn't think they're together, even though they've been sharing a room – and obviously double beds – for the past five weeks. Now Jon thinks maybe Martin is gay. Girls often seem to get very close with gay guys – he's seen it before. It's just a feeling he has – or maybe wishful thinking. When Katrin showed him her photographs, still on her digital camera, he just didn't look like the kind of guy who'd be with Katrin.

Jon wants Katrin to go on the trek with him and Ethan tomorrow. He's decided he likes Hamid and will give him a chance and he's suggesting to Katrin that it'd be great if she came too.

"Mmnnnn, Jon, I am tempted. But I've made a plan with my friends to do a trek with them when they arrive."

"You sure? There are three of them. They'd have no trouble getting a guide."

"But we've been talking about it for a month. I think they'd be hurt, especially as they're probably going to be here in a day or two."

"Have you checked your email."

"The email is down today. The weather's so bad. I'll check again tomorrow."

Jon's mind is ticking over as they speak. If he offered to hang around and wait with her, she'd probably say yes. But he's not sure he wants to go on the trek with Katrin and her friends. What if he's wrong about this Martin guy? What if he is her boyfriend? Then he'd be stuck with them for two whole days. He also doesn't want to seem too keen. Cancelling his plans with Hamid might just scare her off. Jon's mind ticks over as they chat; he can do the trek with Ethan and catch up with Katrin later.

Katrin looks like she is about to ask another question, but she spots Ethan heading for the table. He has a bottle of beer in his hand and an icy glass.

"How goes it?" he says, tossing himself into a chair.

"We've already ordered," says Katrin.

"That's cool. I'll get something in a minute." Ethan doesn't look at Jon as he pours his beer and sucks the head off. Jon will be pissed off, but he doesn't care.

Jon sips on his Coke. He's kept a smile of his face, but he just feels like crying. He doesn't know how to handle this. He knows he's meant to do something. You can't just let a fourteen-year-old drink whenever he feels like it. Not when you're the adult. Not when you're the only one in charge.

But if I try to lay down the law, Jon thinks, he's likely to tell me to fuck off and just keep on drinking. And then what do I do? And now Katrin is seeing this. She must think I'm a total dickhead.

But then Katrin reaches across the table and grabs Ethan's glass. She brings it to her mouth and downs the glass in a long, thirsty gulp. "Very nice. I think I'll have one of my own now," she says. "Jon. Want a beer? Ethan, can I buy you a drink?"

For a second, Jon is stunned into silence.

"Love one," says Ethan quickly.

"Actually, I'm stuffed," says Jon. "Ethan, don't stay up late. We're leaving for the trek tomorrow at eight." He gets up as casually as he can. "Don't let him drink too much," he says to Katrin as he leaves. He's kept the smile on his face the whole time, but he hopes that Ethan and Katrin were listening.

Jon is awake when Ethan stumbles in three hours later. The power is out, but that's no excuse for the loud trip as one of his feet collects his backpack or for the cursing. Jon knows Ethan has had more than just a beer or two. And as he passes by Jon's bed on the way to the toilet, Jon smells cigarettes. Indonesian clove cigarettes.

He lies in his sleep sheet listening to the rain falling on the roof and to Ethan's racket as he tries to find the toilet in the dark. There's a "Fuck!" muttered with pain. A stubbed toe, perhaps? Then another clatter and then the churning sound of Ethan's loud, rushing beer piss.

Jon lies motionless as Ethan picks his way back past him to the bed, flopping noisily into it, breathing heavily as he struggles to find the opening to his sleep sheet and get his strangely uncoordinated limbs inside it. He tosses and turns, but its only minutes before his breathing settles into the rhythm of sleep and then falls into an ugly piggish snore. Deep, nasal, faltering.

And awfully familiar.

Jon is standing by her bed, his face wet from the nightmare. The light from the street lamp bathes the room in light, throwing his shadow across the rumpled bed and her big, motionless form. His feet are cold on the floor and he's shivering violently. He calls her softly. Then a little louder. He even shakes her arm. Gently. But she won't wake. Then her eyes flutter open. They are watery slits, glistening as the light catches them, but dull and lifeless. Did she even see him? She closes her eyes again. Now he's afraid to try again.

For the third time today, Jon feels tears behind his eyes and a crushing constriction in his throat. He won't give in to it. Turning his back on Ethan, he draws his knees up to his chest and tunes his ears towards the jungle noises, the roar of the river and the driving tropical rain.

6

Gunung Leuser National Park

They've been walking, on and off, for four hours and Ethan is sick of it. It hasn't even looked like stopping raining. He's drenched to the skin and has slipped over so many times, he's completely plastered in mud. His shorts are starting to chafe. Every step he takes hurts. He's started walking with his hand permanently tugging at his groin holding the wet fabric away from his skin. It'd be humiliating if anyone sees, but he's walking at the back and Jon and Hamid couldn't be less interested in him. They're moving faster and they keep getting miles ahead and out of sight.

For long periods of time he's been totally on his own, just the steady hum of jungle noises and the rhythmic clump-squelch, clump-squelch of his feet hitting the muddy trail.

And he hasn't seen a single animal. Unless you count bugs – which he doesn't. Millions of ants, ugly centipedes, mosquitos the size of blowflies. But no animals. Not the big ones Jon had gone on about. Orang-utans, tigers, even rhinos.

Mind you, he's not sure when he's supposed to look for all these animals. The whole time he's having to trudge on to keep up, and it's obvious that taking his eyes off where he's putting his feet would be really dumb. It's not only slippery with mud. There are loose stones, that take the ground out from under him, logs, branches and tangled vines across the trail to trip over and holes that appear suddenly and look designed to break his leg. And, though he hasn't seen one, he knows that there are poisonous snakes including king cobras. Out here he knows if he is bitten, he'll die. So he keeps his eyes down.

And Jon still isn't talking to him. In fact he has spent the whole four hours walking off ahead with Hamid, talking Indonesian with him, making sure Ethan is totally left out. It's been pretty obvious. There was barely a word said this morning when he got up.

And for at least the last two hours he's hardly seen Jon at all. They've stopped waiting for him, altogether. He's not sure when he last saw them – maybe a half hour ago? He hadn't looked at the time. Ethan's getting irritated and more than a little concerned. What if he'd hurt himself, or wandered off the track? What is to say that he hasn't already gotten lost? Except he knows they're ahead of him. Jon and Hamid's shoe prints have been in the mud ahead of him all along the way and they're still there. The rain must have washed away others from days before, leaving just the two. And he's been using them as a kind of guide map – step here – don't step there – look at that slide mark.

He'd like to be appreciating the jungle. There's no doubt that it's awesome. Nothing like he's ever seen in Australia, even when the school took them to the Dandenongs for a picnic. That was pretty cool – really different from his neighbourhood. But this jungle is just immense. It rises up and up, enormous trees reaching skyward, looking for sun shine, but smothered in by a dense canopy of vines and other growth. It's so dense it's impossible to see where one plant finishes and the next one starts.

Soon the path heads downwards, maybe fifty metres, and starts to follow a rougher, narrower trail along the steep banks of a river. The path is all up and down now, scrambling over and under trees and logs. Ethan grimaces as he has to take his protective hand from his shorts, catching a tree branch to stop himself skidding down a muddy gully straight into the churning water. He has to concentrate hard now, picking each move carefully, using both hands and feet as he holds onto roots embedded in the river bank or vines to keep from sliding off the path altogether.

He's not sure what river this is. It must be thirty metres across and it's very swollen. It looks as big as – maybe bigger – than the Bohorok River they'd crossed that morning to head into the jungle. Who knows, maybe it's the same river and they've met it again further upstream. It's moving quickly, with white caps indicating submerged obstacles. The noise is deafening. A crashing roar that drowns out the background jungle noises Ethan has become used to. Immediately he realises his nerves are on edge. More than once he's seen large branches and even small trees being swept down the river like the one that had nearly wiped out his canoe yesterday. In places the rising river has taken the old path and he's seen where Hamid and Jon have made a new one straight through the jungle, above the water line.

Because of the noise of the river and his intense concentration on picking his path, he doesn't realise he has caught up to Jon and Hamid until he stumbles upon them. Both are perched on a large fallen log, Jon sipping on bottled water, Hamid smoking a cigarette. They are chatting in Indonesian and Jon doesn't look at him as he arrives.

As soon as he gets there, it seems the rest time is over. When am I meant to take a rest, thinks Ethan?

Just around the corner the path stops by another enormous tree that has fallen across the river. It's obviously been there for a long time. All the bark and most of the branches have broken away, leaving a smooth white trunk, maybe fifty metres long and three quarters of a metre in diameter. It spans the entire width of the river, clearing the swirling water by a good metre at its lowest point.

Hamid jumps up onto the log. It's clearly slippery and he positions his feet so that one gains purchase against a large knot. "*Hati-hati!*" he says. "Be careful! It is better for you to go over on this." Hamid turns side on and sticks his arse out dramatically, tapping it with his hand and laughing. He then squats down and straddles the tree, one leg either side. Using his hands in front, he leans forward, taking his weight on his hands like a rabbit and pulls himself forward. Repeating the motion he bum-hops along the tree for a metre or two, looking at Jon and Ethan to be sure they understand. "Very safe," he says brightly. Then, ignoring his own advice, he scrambles back to his feet and walks carefully, like a tightrope walker, out to the middle of the river and stands there waiting.

Ethan doesn't fancy sliding fifty metres along a tree with his groin already rubbed half raw with the chaffing. "You go," he says to Jon.

"No, you." Jon is still avoiding looking at him.

Suddenly Ethan's feeling really pissed with Jon. And feeling pissed has always stopped him feeling scared. He knows he could walk fifty metres across a tree trunk if it were just lying on the ground. Ethan's done that sort of thing plenty of times. He has good balance and there is no way he'd normally fall if he really tried not to. He can do it – just long as he doesn't look past the log to the water.

Ethan kicks at his shoes. They are caked in mud and that will make them slippery. He scratches at the tread with a stick, then rinses them in a puddle. Then, before Jon has a chance to object, he's on the log and walking across. He takes the first few steps quickly, then as he reaches the start of the river he slows, picking his steps carefully, arms outstretched, keeping balance.

He is relieved. It is easy. But it's also slippery. The log's surface is worn smooth and sopping wet. Hamid's shoes have muddied it up too, which doesn't help. Ethan has to concentrate.

But then his mind wanders, just for a moment and his eyes glance past the log to the water below and he immediately wobbles, losing balance for a second.

Focus on the log only, he tells himself. He hears Jon yelling at him to sit down. He ignores him, then blocks him out. Out of the corner of his eye he sees Hamid still perched in the middle of the log. Ethan hopes he moves before he gets there because he doesn't want to stop and have an argument with him.

Hamid waits until Ethan is about five metres short of him, then he heads off himself keeping the distance between the two. It only takes a minute and both of them are safely across the river.

"That was cool," says Ethan. He's feeling really pleased with himself. Now he's across he can look back, refocus on the danger of the river and get really excited. He takes his pack off and finds his camera, carefully wrapped in plastic bags. "Hamid, take my photo?" he asks.

Hamid reaches for the camera, wiping his hands on his wet clothes.

"What are you doing?" It's Jon, still on the other bank.

He's yelling really loudly to be heard over the river, but Ethan pretends he can't hear him. He walks about ten metres back along the log, then turns around. "Take lots," he calls to Hamid. It's digital so he wants a selection to choose from. He slowly walks the log back to Hamid, looking up as much as he can for the photos.

Back on land again, he takes the camera and quickly looks at the digital images. They're good, but it's still raining so he puts the camera back in the plastic as soon as he can. Maybe Jon wants a photo. If so, he can ask nicely when he gets here, thinks Ethan.

Jon still isn't on the log and for the first time Ethan starts to think he might be scared.

"Come on, it's easy!" he calls. On the surface, he's meaning to encourage Jon, but at the same time he knows he's probably also being a bit of a prick and needling him. If Jon really doesn't want to walk over, telling him it's easy is going to piss him off big time.

Jon's still not on the log. He's taking forever. Ethan had barely given Jon a thought when he decided to walk across – maybe a little silent "Stuff you, I'll do what I want" thought – but really he just didn't want to rub himself any rawer by sliding his groin over that tree trunk. But now he sees he's put Jon in a bit of a position. If Jon goes over on his bum now, when they have gone on their feet, he's going to look like a real chicken.

And Ethan knows Jon doesn't like heights. He's not phobic, but nor is he really comfortable. Jon had hated the chairlift that time, when he took Ethan to the Royal Melbourne Show. And he's also ridiculously tall and thin. Just the wrong shape for balancing, not nuggetty and compact like Ethan and Hamid.

Suddenly Jon is on his feet and walking slowly, but confidently across the log. He's doing OK, thinks Ethan. He's not a natural like Hamid, but he's doing OK and he's pretty quick. Jon is halfway across and going strong.

Then it all happens incredibly quickly. Out of the corner of his eye Ethan catches sight of something huge moving down the river.

Hamid sees it too and cries out, "*Hati-hati!*" just as Ethan screams, "Look out!"

There's no time to brace themselves. Just before impact, Ethan realises it is a wave. A white wall of water half a metre high, churning up spray another two metres and carrying a tree with branches and roots still attached. It's heading for the log bridge.

Jon drops to his knees, then hugs the log. The wave goes whooshing underneath, with the roots end of the floating tree missing him by centimetres. The branches of the tree strike the bridge about fifteen metres from Jon. There's a gigantic splash that showers Jon and the bridge in water. For a second Ethan thinks it's been ripped right off the bank and that Jon's gone with it, swept down the river. Then, in an instant, it's over. The floating tree is gone, the bridge remains. Through the fine mist that hangs in the air, Ethan can see that Jon is still there, on his belly hugging the bridge with arms and legs.

Ethan is so shaken he can't speak. Jon must be OK or he'd have fallen off the log. He knows that, but still he cannot speak. Hamid is quicker to react. He's out there in a second, but even he's lost his nerve. Now he's on his arse skimming over to Jon. Ethan watches as the two of them talk for a moment. Then Hamid turns round and comes back, on his arse as quickly as he can. Jon follows.

Minutes later Ethan still hasn't said a word. Jon is fine. He's making jokes about how he can't stop his hands from shaking. And it's true. They're shaking like he's got a fever. He's sitting down and a couple of times he tries to stand, but his legs are still wobbly and he's laughing about that too. Hamid thinks it's hysterical. He's totally wired, his conversation darting between Indonesian and English, hand gestures re-enacting the collision every few seconds. Soon he's got a cigarette out and this seems to settle him down.

Jon's making jokes about how he wished he was a smoker at times like this. He's picked up a twig and is pretending to smoke it, and the two of them are laughing at how much Jon's hand is shaking. Ethan's not feeling any better. Seeing Jon like this just freaks him out more. Hamid wouldn't know it, but Jon's really shaken. He hates smoking with such a passion, he'd never normally joke about it.

Ethan's half watching them, but he can't take his eyes off the river. After the wave went through, the water level never completely fell. It is definitely higher than before. At its lowest point, it is now almost lapping against the log bridge.

"Hey, fellas! Have a look at this," he calls.

"Is this a problem, Hamid?" Jon asks.

"Maybe," says Hamid. "Maybe tomorrow we come back and bridge under water. Or maybe another big tree come down river and take bridge away."

"Is there another way across?"

"No. Not near here. You must…" he makes signals showing how they'd have to slash through the jungle. "Very far from here. No path."

"We should go back, then," says Jon.

Ethan feels a momentary stab of happiness. He'd love a hot shower, dry clothes, a dry bed.

"It is too far to walk back before dark," says Hamid, dashing Ethan's hopes.

"I don't mean go back to Bukit Lawang. I just mean that we should stay on the other side. So we don't get trapped. We can still camp out."

"But everything is sopping wet. We're not even going to be able to have a fire." Ethan's trying, but even he can hear the tired, whiny tone in his voice. He decides to keep his mouth shut.

"Hamid has plenty of food. We don't need a fire. We'll be fine. And I still want to see a tiger," Jon's enthusiasm is back.

"Who is going first?" says Hamid pointing at the log.

"I am," says Jon. "And I'm going to spend as little time out there as I possibly can."

It's pitch-black and still raining. A tarpaulin is stretched out above them, shielding them from direct rainfall, but they're all sopping wet anyway.

Jon is sitting up, wide awake. He's heard something in the jungle. Something large. Ethan and Hamid are asleep and he doesn't wake them. He won't – not until he's sure.

He has a torch, but he won't use it until he's got a pretty good idea that he'll see something. Sightings of the Sumatran tiger are incredibly rare – so few are left in the wild and they avoid humans as best as they can. If this is a tiger, he'll be incredibly lucky. Hamid said he'd seen one once two years before and he's in the jungle all the time. And to see one here would be incredible. It's within four hours walk of Bukit Lawang and the surrounding villages. Normally you'd have to travel much further into the jungle to hope to see one. But maybe with this weather the tiger's behaviour has changed. There are definitely fewer people about. And Hamid fell asleep pretty soon after the sun set. Maybe that's why he hasn't seen more of them. He sleeps instead of staying awake.

Jon can still hear it. It's moving through the undergrowth. Just the swish of wet branches against a large body, the muffled crackle of damp twigs bending under the weight of mighty paws gently placed. It's not getting closer or further away. Is it moving past parallel to them? Or circling them? His heart is pounding in his chest, but it is excitement, not fear. He doesn't see the tiger as a threat, though he knows it could kill all three of them if it wanted.

His thumb hovers over the torch button. If he senses it retreating, he'll flick it on straight away, but for now he waits, willing it to come in closer.

He holds his breath. He doesn't want to frighten it. The irony strikes him, momentarily. For thousands of years humans have feared tigers. But now the hunter has become the hunted. It is humans who slip back and forth across the boundaries between the villages and the jungle, stalking, trapping, killing. Nature has been turned on its head. The mighty tiger is safe nowhere.

Jon tries to push the thought away. He doesn't want to spoil this experience.

He hears the animal stop. It can't be more than twenty metres away, on the edge of the clearing he remembers from when it was light. Is it taking cover in the last of the foliage? Has it smelt them? He thinks he can hear its breath, but maybe he's imagining it. The noises of the jungle are much greater at night. Jon places his hand on his brother's shoulder, then feels upwards until he find his mouth. Covering it, he shakes Ethan and clamps hard on his mouth as he stirs and tries to pull his head away.

Leaning across, he whispers, "Quiet! It's a tiger."

Ethan is immediately alert and motionless. Jon removes his hand and Ethan slowly pulls his body into a seated position, careful to minimise noise.

Ethan brings his face right up to Jon's ear. "Where?" he whispers.

Jon hears the tension in the whisper and is satisfied to recognise Ethan's fear mixed with excitement. He reaches down and takes his brother's hand, lifting it and pointing it in the direction he had last sensed the tiger's movement.

For at least a minute they sit there silently and motionlessly, staring blindly into the blackness, their ears straining for the slightest sound above the steady jungle noises.

Then Hamid stirs in his sleep, mutters something and rolls over. Instantly there is the noise of something moving. Jon has the torch on and he flicks it across the foliage, searching, anxious not to miss the moment.

And there it is. For a second or two. A tiger. They see its whole body, head, limbs, tail. Its stripes are stark and bold, but colourless in the torch light. In fact everything – the tiger, the foliage – everything – is grey-scale – like night vision in a war movie. Just then the animal's eyes flash brightly as it turns its head, catching the torch light. There is a blur of movement and it is gone.

Jon and Ethan sit there for quite a while as if they might get it to come back. Then when it is clear it is gone, Ethan swears softly several times.

"Cool, huh?" says Jon softly. He is still using the torch, lighting up the jungle canopy, carefully looking for other animals.

"Should we wake Hamid?"

"Nah," says Jon. "It's gone and he's missed it. He won't thank us for waking him. He's lucky he's able to sleep sopping wet on this hard ground."

"I won't be able to sleep now."

"Then wake me if you hear anything." Jon lays down and plonks the torch next to Ethan.

"I need a piss," says Ethan.

"Well, go on," says Jon.

"But there's a tiger out there."

For some reason Jon is pleased by Ethan's nervousness. "Don't worry about it. It's gone," he says.

"How do you know?"

"Want me to hold your hand?"

"Fuck off!" Ethan hisses – softly so as to not wake Hamid.

But he still hasn't got up. So Jon grabs the torch and scrambles to his feet. "Come on. I'll have a look for its paw prints in the mud, while you mark out your territory."

7

The Jungle Inn

"Can you believe this?" Katrin seems very worked up about something. "All day yesterday it rained, so I became very bored and lots of times I went to try the email and then, for just a few minutes, the email is up. There's a message from my friends, who are still in Malaysia. Can you believe this? They won't be here for ten more days!"

"So you could have done the trek with us," says Ethan.

"I should have. Now I have to find things to do for ten days and return if I want to see my friends and trek in the Gunung Leuser National Park. It was worth it?"

"Awesome," says Ethan. He's already told her about the tiger.

"So what do you plan to do for the next ten days? Stay here?" Jon isn't trying to keep the coolness out of his voice.

Ethan is puzzled. Since the encounter with the tiger last night, Jon had been in a much better mood. But now, back with Katrin, he's lost his sense of humour again.

Katrin's pizza arrives. It's the strangest thing Ethan's ever seen. There's a high pastry shell, like a pie case without a lid. It's baked hard like biscuit. On the inside is a deep pool of runny tomato soup with a few dollops of melted cheese floating about.

She looks a little surprised, but then breaks off a piece of the crust. Like the breaking of a dam wall, tomato soup runs out spreading over the plate. Katrin dabs at the bloody-looking flood with the pastry, then pops it in her mouth. From the expression on her face it must taste OK.

She takes a long sip of her fruit shake. "I can't stand it here any more," she says. "It's so wet I feel like now my whole room is damp. It's in my mattress and none of my clothes will dry. Even out of the rain there's so much humidity, they're still sopping after three days."

"Want to climb a volcano?" says Ethan.

"I have already. At last count I've climbed four, just in Indonesia. But as this country has about four hundred, I guess there's plenty more. Which one do you have in mind?"

"Sib… Sib… Hey, Jon, what's the name of that volcano?"

"Gunung Sibayak."

"At Berstagi?" says Katrin. "Yes, I had hoped to go there if I have time. But I have only three weeks here in Sumatra and have to be back in ten days to see my friends. And I also wanted to go to Lake Toba."

"We're going there too. We're only going to Berstagi for three nights. Maybe four. That gives you four or five days at Toba."

"Wanna Coke, Ethan?" says Jon standing.

"Ta, mate," says Ethan.

"Drink, Katrin?"

"No thanks."

When Jon is out or earshot, Katrin asks, "Is Jon OK?"

"Yeah, he's fine. Don't worry about him. We had a bit of an argument, but he'll get over it."

"I feel he's upset with me."

"Na. It's me. Forget it. He's just a bit of me at the moment."

"Why?"

"He's got this crazy idea that I'm some kind of teenage alcoholic."

"Why does he think that?"

"Well, partly he's paranoid. Before Mum got sick she was a bit of a drinker. 'Cause of that Jon's really off drinking. Apart from a beer on a hot day he barely touches alcohol."

"But you do?"

"Back home a lot of kids my age have a few drinks. Mum never worried about it – I don't see why he should care."

"Sounds like he's just being careful. You're only fourteen and he's got to make sure you're OK."

Jon is back with the Cokes. "No ice," he says to Ethan, placing the Coke bottle and a glass on the table. "'Cause of the power being out."

"Yes, it's not come on at all this morning," says Katrin. "I'd be very careful with the food. Don't order anything with meat. Anything that should be refrigerated."

"You mean like cheese?" says Ethan pointing to the pizza soup.

"I think this is OK," says Katrin. "The cheese here is probably one of those long-life one's that are kept on the shelf."

The glass looks clean so Ethan pours the Coke. In Indonesia, soft drink is mainly sold in bottles that have been recycled dozens of times. Cans are available, but they are very expensive because they're not so easily recycled. Only wealthy Indonesians would buy a can ahead of a bottle.

This recycling of bottles can be a little worrying as you're meant to be constantly concerned about getting sick from poor hygiene. Bottled soft drink is meant to be safe, but you've got to worry about who exactly is doing the bottling. Sometimes Coke turns up in a Fanta bottle and vice versa. It can be a bit unnerving. This particular bottle is old and scratched and has obviously been recycled many times over. The cap has been removed, but the bottle neck has grime caked around it. No way he'd drink from the bottle, but out of the glass he figures it's fine. Probably.

"Hey, Jon! Ethan!" It's Hamid. He's got a couple of other young guys with him.

"Hey, Hamid! You all dried out yet?" says Ethan.

"I bring my friends to meet the tourists who saw the tiger. Hopefully you tell all the tourists that I took you somewhere with tigers."

Ethan's pleased to help. "Katrin, Hamid took us somewhere with tigers," he says.

"You want trek?" Hamid asks hopefully.

"Thank you, but not in this weather," answers Katrin.

"Very wet," agrees Hamid. "Hey, these my friends from Bohorok Village." He points to each of the young men in turn, introducing them. They shake hands politely and say hello, but none seems very confident while the conversation is in English.

"I'll be going," says Jon a little later. He waves to Ethan, Katrin, Hamid and his friends, drains the last of his Coke and heads for the door.

"Jon, not just yet. Please stay a minute," says Katrin.

"Why?"

"I want to talk to you. Today I feel you are upset."

"I'm fine. I'm tired. I'm gunna lie down for a while." Jon has kept walking and Katrin follows him out the door.

They stand for a moment under the awning as rain pours off the roof onto the ground.

"You don't seem fine. You seem angry with me and I'm not sure what I've done."

"Don't worry about it."

"Of course I'll worry. Come over to my room. There's a table and chairs under cover. We can sit there and talk." She grabs his arm once and squeezes it. "Got a torch?"

He nods in response.

She flicks hers on and runs off into the night, splashing her way across to cover. Jon follows.

"So, Jon, Ethan says you're angry with him because he drank too much. But why are you angry with me?"

Jon looks like he's going to pretend she's imagining things, but then he changes his mind. "It's like this," he says. "I know Europeans all have a different attitude to drinking alcohol, but I didn't like you getting Ethan drunk the other night."

"What do you mean?"

"Well, you all have wine with lunch and dinner as children, don't you?"

"Many families, yes. But we don't allow our children to get drunk. Quite the opposite. We try to model responsible approaches to alcohol, by allowing them a glass with food. And we don't abuse alcohol ourselves in front of them. At least, my family never did and neither do the people I know."

"So you're saying there are no European alcoholics?"

"No, of course not! Always there are some. But I think Australians have a bigger reputation for abusing alcohol than Europeans. And…" Katrin takes a deep breath. She is feeling increasingly angry with Jon. "And, for your information, I bought one beer for Ethan to replace his when I drank it. Then both of us went to bed."

"He came in drunk hours later."

"He left the Jungle Inn with me and walked me to my room. This was about twenty minutes after you went to bed. Maybe he went back on his own."

Jon drops his face in his hands. Obviously she was telling the truth. He's feeling embarrassed, relieved and worried all at the same time. "Katrin – I'm sorry. When you bought him that drink and stayed with him and then he came home drunk, I just assumed he was with you."

"Well, he wasn't. And I probably wouldn't have left him there drinking either. As I said, I thought he was going back to the room."

"I hate the thought of him choosing to drink alone even more." That's what Mum did, Jon thinks. She'd drink with company if someone was around, but mostly she drank by herself.

"Maybe he was with some of Hamid's friends."

"Most of them don't drink. They're Muslims."

"Some are Christian. They don't mind a beer, though they can't afford to drink it usually."

"I'll have to keep an eye on him," says Jon. "But I'm not his father. How do I stop him?"

"The same way a father would, I guess."

"I never had one," says Jon. "And what if he just defies me? What if he just says 'No'?"

"You can't be afraid to set your boundaries just because you worry what will happen if you can't enforce them. You must be firm about what you expect from him."

"And if he just ignores me?"

"Think of some consequences."

"Like what? Parents on TV only ever seem to ground their kids when they do the wrong thing. But we're travelling. How do I ground him here?"

"Use your imagination. Instead of grounding him, you don't go to Lake Toba – if that is something he's looking forward to. Or if you're going to let him have an occasional beer with you, you take away the privilege if he abuses it and drinks when you're not there. Or you don't give him his own money. He'll hate that, but you are his guardian. It is your choice. Or maybe – as a bottom line – you have to take him home. Back to Australia."

"It all sounds so easy when you say it," laughs Jon.

"Actually, I'm sure it's terrifying," says Katrin. "But you should also remember that Ethan wants your approval. It's not just about wielding a big stick."

Jon looks doubtful. "If he wanted my approval he wouldn't get drunk when he knows I hate it and then throw it in my face."

"Don't be so sure you know what's going on in his head. Maybe fear of losing your approval is stopping him from drinking to excess constantly, if he has a real urge to do so. Your mother abused alcohol. Maybe Ethan has that tendency too. And maybe you are actually helping him to control it, although not perfectly. If he weren't with you, he might be much, much worse. In Europe we have many teenagers of fourteen and younger who live on the streets."

"We have them in Australia too." In truth that had always been Jon's real fear. That if he let Ethan go into foster care, he'd go right off the rails, run away, get in with the wrong crowd and ultimately end up on the streets, a drug addict or a drunk like his mother.

"Maybe you are the reason he has not gone down that path already."

"It still feels like he's throwing it in my face and doing it deliberately to disrespect me."

"It feels that way because you're frustrated."

Jon shrugs. "Maybe," he says.

"Exactly how did he throw it in your face? All he did was come home after he got drunk. Did you expect him to go sleep in the jungle so as not to confront you?"

"Of course not!

"And when he came home, did he wake you up and taunt you?"

Jon smiled. "No, he slunk into bed without a word, thinking I was asleep and hoping I wouldn't notice, I guess."

"See?"

Jon smiles. "You've got a point, I guess."

"Now, are you happy I'm coming to Berstagi to climb the volcano?"

"Of course," says Jon. "Let's hope the weather there is better than this."

8

Berstagi

Sunshine, for the first day in a week. Even though it's late afternoon and they're stranded by the side of the road, ten kilometres out of town, at least they're not cold and sopping wet.

But why won't any of these buses stop? About ten have gone past them in the past twenty minutes. They've tried to flag them down – increasingly desperately each time – but the buses just hoot their horns, the passengers packed inside and on the roof cheer and wave and the buses just go on by.

What is with them? They are all obviously full inside – never has Jon seen so many people jammed into public transport – but there is still room on the roof. Each bus has had fifteen to twenty men sitting up there along with sacks of rice, baskets of vegetables, bicycles and who knows what else. This is perfectly normal for Sumatra and he has almost gotten used to seeing it. There are ladders up the sides of the buses to help people get up and down again.

Maybe it is because they are tourists, Jon thinks. Another bus sails past, this one with a custom horn so loud it almost blasts them off the road. Again the ten or so men on the roof wave in a friendly fashion.

"Stop!" cries Ethan, who's beginning to lose his temper.

"It's because of me," says Katrin at last.

Of course. Jon could have kicked himself. Only men ride on the roof. He vaguely remembers hearing about this. Indonesia has lots of symbolism and customs related to the head. A woman sitting above the head of a man would be a sign of disrespect. So only men get to sit on the roof. If the inside is full, bad luck. He explains his theory to Katrin and Ethan.

"Yes, yes. I think that makes sense," says Katrin. "Or maybe it's seen as undignified for women, like sitting with your legs apart is in Western culture."

"Or spitting," says Ethan.

"Yes, you would never see a woman spit in public in Belgium, but in Sumatra we see it often."

"So what do we do?" Jon says.

"How about I hide back here?" Katrin gestures to a large tree by the roadside. You and Ethan flag one down. When it stops I'll run over."

"Then what? You'll defy Sumatran sense of decency and climb up on top?"

"Maybe. We'll see. Let's just get the bus to stop first."

It doesn't take long. Just a few minutes. The next bus that comes along pulls up just a few metres from Jon and Ethan. They jog over and Ethan latches onto one of the ladders that hang down the side of the bus. He starts to climb quickly.

When he's halfway up, Jon calls, "Come on, Katrin!"

She slips out from behind the tree and runs to the ladder. Jon waits, ready to help her up.

Immediately there's a commotion from inside and on top. Jon can't pick up the words, but the tone is clear. They're doing something wrong. He looks up and there are men at the top of the ladder holding up their hands signalling Ethan to stop. He's near the top of the ladder but the men on top are not going to let him up.

The conductor is beside him. He's just a little fella. About five feet three, with longish straight hair that hangs down over his eyes and a smoke hanging out of his mouth. He's none too pleased.

Jon smiles his most innocent smile. "*Mengapa?* Why?" he says, although he knows perfectly well what the problem is.

The conductor wrenches the smoke from between his teeth and says something, but it's either too fast or it's not Indonesian – maybe the local Batak language – and Jon doesn't get it. The kid looks little older than Ethan, Jon thinks, but he's full of confidence and knows his job. And he's got an attitude a mile wide. The smoke is back in the mouth, but hand gestures and expressions make the message clear. Indicating Katrin, he shakes his head firmly.

Jon tries out his Indonesian. "*Tetapi kami harus ke Berstagi.* But we must get to Berstagi.'

Out comes the smoke again.

"*Bis lain! Bis lain!* Another bus! Another bus!' A cloud of grey smoke swirls around his face. The bus is revving its engines and he's in a hurry to get going.

Jon persists. "*Semua bis lain penuh juga.* All the other buses are also full.'

There are voices from within the bus. Heads poke out the glassless windows and there is a huge racket. Many people are smiling. They're clearly curious and enjoying the drama.

A woman calls something out to the young man. The bus roars with laughter, but it's clearly not complimentary and he doesn't see the joke. Jon wishes he understood, but it's not any kind of Indonesian he knows. Then there's a whole bunch of commotion inside and two women slip out the door followed by a gnarled ancient old man with only one leg. The conductor rushes to his side and helps him down, then a crutch is pushed out the door and handed to the conductor, who hands it up to the men on the roof. The conductor waves to Ethan to climb and the men on the roof move to allow him up. The old man grabs the ladder with his hands and the conductor places a hand on his bum. The old man uses his one foot, his hands and the conductor's firm pressure on his backside to haul himself up until men on the roof can lean down and pull him the rest of the way.

The conductor ushers Katrin towards the door of the bus and she is squeezed inside. Seeing her safely on board, Jon skims up the ladder as the bus takes off.

Up on top, no one seems to bear a grudge about the trick they'd tried or the climb they'd caused the poor old man. In fact, the old man seems to bask in the fuss of the moment. He's smiling a big toothless grin. Taking his crutch, he prods Ethan on the leg, then makes some comment that everyone finds funny. They're a laugh-a-minute bunch, these Sumatrans.

Jon feels a tap on the shoulder and he turns.

A guy about his age is grinning at him. "*Rokok?*" he asks. He's asking for a smoke.

Jon grins back. "*Maaf, tidak merokok.* Sorry, I don't smoke.'

He feels another tap from another side. Another man, a little older. He's holding out a piece of fruit, which Jon knows is called *salak*. It has a skin like snake skin and inside it is segmented, a bit like a mandarin, but with the texture more like apple.

Jon nods, smiles and reaches to pull off a segment. He pops it in his mouth and chews, carefully extracting the large seed and tossing it from the roof of the bus. Though he isn't sure he likes it, he says, "*Enak.* Delicious," and everyone laughs.

From behind him he feels a hand come around his biceps, fingers squeezing, feeling the muscle. It's an unusual kind of touch and not what he'd normally expect from a man. Jon swings his head around, half expecting to see Katrin. But it's another guy about his age. He too grins at Jon, his dark brown eyes friendly and full of humour. Jon feels his fingers lingering over Jon's arm trailing across his skin. It feels sexual to Jon, like he's is making a pass at him, but he knows in his head he isn't.

Then the guy flexes his own biceps to show Jon.

"*Kuat sekali*! Very strong!" says Jon and the guy roars with laughter and slaps him on the shoulder.

Soon there's someone else's hand on his leg and another tap on the shoulder, an offer of a banana, and an offer – this time – of a smoke. There are maybe fifteen men and boys up here, including Ethan and himself and most of the Indonesians close to him seem to be keen on touching him, one way or another. He's trying to be casual about this, although it's crowding him a bit and making him just a little uncomfortable. He knows they're just curious and friendly. Indonesian men are very affectionate to each other. He's almost stopped noticing teenage guys, or even middle-aged men walking arm in arm or holding hands, it's just so ordinary here.

Out of the corner of his eye he sees Ethan with a kretek cigarette in his mouth, blowing smoke out his nose. Jon decides to ignore it. He's trying to be smarter about what he says to Ethan. He may hate smoking but, if Ethan chooses to do it, there's nothing he can really do to stop him. From now on he's going to pick his battles.

It's only a few minutes before the roof passengers are used to him and they settle down and go back to whatever they were doing. Some are obviously farmers, complete with tools, coming home from the fields. Jon's found himself a comfortable and secure spot, wedged against some sturdy metal bars bolted to the roof of the bus. It's near the edge, though, which allows him a great view of the activity.

As the bus reaches the outskirts of Berstagi, people begin to get off and on, and newcomers join them on the roof. Jon is mesmerised by the young conductor, who has so much energy he seems to be on drugs. While the bus is in motion, he is constantly clambering about the outside of the bus like a rock climber, his feet on metal rungs and ladders. After each stop he makes his way to wherever newcomers have found a spot, his hand gripping tightly as he reaches inside to collect fares from inside passengers through the glassless windows. Periodically he scales the ladders and collects fares from new arrivals on the roof, then he is down the other side to take fares through the windows along the other side of the bus. When the bus slows to stop, he jumps down to help load and unload the roof, often having to jog along side to jump back on as it starts up again. The whole time, the kid rarely shuts up, when he's not calling out something, he's singing away loudly in a toneless voice. It looks like great fun – even Jon can see that.

Ethan too is enjoying the ride. He loves the feeling of the wind on his face and the three-hundred-and-sixty-degree view of the world whirling by as he flies through the tree tops on the roof of a speeding bus. No one at school would believe this. He'd love to be up here with a video camera. Better still he'd like to strap a video camera to the head of that kid who's doing the monkey-man impersonation on the outside of the bus. It'd be like those films they made down the skate park last summer.

Maybe he'll ask Jon about getting some cameras and making a little film. He could show it at school next year. Maybe in Indonesian. Be a lot more interesting than learning how to say "My father is a doctor" or "My mother is a teacher." He'd not liked Indonesian much and hadn't made a friend of the teacher when he asked her how to say, "I don't know who my father is" and "My mother's a junkie." She wasn't. Not then, anyway. But then he was just trying to stir the teacher. And even he was hardly likely to make a joke out of cancer.

Ethan's had a good day, but he's kind of tired now and he's glad to be able to just sit back and let the world go by.

They'd arrived in Berstagi about lunchtime, already stuffed. The bad weather had lead to the supposed cancellation of bus services from Bukit Lawang and in the end they'd had to charter their own minibus to get out. It might have been another tourist scam – the guide book actually mentions that this happens all the time – but faced with staying there another day in the never ending downpour, they'd looked the other way and paid for convenience.

After about four hours of wild dodgem driving, the minibus pulled up in Berstagi outside a guest house, the Elshaddai, with whom the drivers clearly had some arrangement. Another scam? Who knows? And who cares? It was a good hotel. The rooms were clean and basic – just a double bed in each and a shared bathroom, but they were incredibly cheap – only two dollars a night. As far as he could tell, the place was empty apart from them. Katrin took a room on the second floor overlooking the street.

Ethan was really surprised when Jon offered to pay so he and Ethan could have a room each.

"It's so cheap," he said. "We could probably both use a bit of space and I don't fancy sharing that little double bed with you. Besides, the hotel owner looks pretty desperate for business. Must be really hard since the tourists started avoiding Indonesia."

It's plain to see how badly tourism is doing in Sumatra. Everywhere Ethan has been he's seen signs of a once thriving tourist industry that is now in its death throes. So much has gone wrong here in the last five or six years. First, enormous forest fires in Malaysia and Indonesia had led to huge areas, including the whole of Sumatra and much of Malaysia, being blanketed in thick choking smoke for months on end. The tourists stayed away in droves. Then in the north of Sumatra there was an upsurge in conflict over the Acehnese wanting to be independent of Indonesia. Although tourists had not been targeted, at times there had been open conflict. Then in October the previous year the bombing of tourists in Bali had further put people off travelling in Indonesia. People trying to make a living in tourism were doing it very tough.

With the whole afternoon to kill, Katrin had suggested they go see a waterfall just out of town. That's how they'd found themselves stranded by the roadside.

It had been one problem after another: a continuation of the morning transport dramas. They'd made their way to the bus stop in Berstagi. Like the one in Medan, it was huge. Just a large square of open land, maybe a hundred metres across with dozens of buses parked around the perimeter. People were everywhere, selling, buying, getting on and off buses, loading their roofs with the most amazing stuff.

He'd stopped to watch as a couple of men lift about five motorcycles onto the roof of a bus. First they stood a bike on its back wheel and raised it as high as they could. A man on top leaned over, holding on with one hand and with the other looping a hand through the front wheel. Lifting it a little, a second man on the roof caught hold and the two of them hauled it up. It took less than thirty seconds to load each motorbike – these guys looked like they did this everyday.

He had been glad it was Jon and Katrin who were doing all the work trying to find the bus. The first person they'd asked had smiled and waved vaguely towards a row of buses on the other side. They'd gone over there and someone else had sent them back again. Two or three others waved them to completely different places. He could see Jon getting frustrated but trying not to show it, keeping a big smile on his face and a gentle tone in his voice. Jon had told him that in Indonesia it is considered very rude to become angry or aggressive and that no one will ever help you if you lose your cool.

After about half a confusing hour they managed to find the bus they thought was the right one. It was nearly full, but three tiny seats were found for them inside. Ethan was squashed up against a wrinkly, nearly-toothless Indonesian lady wearing a traditional brown sarong and blouse. When she opened her mouth it was stained bright red – from chewing betel nut, Katrin explained. She sat between him and Jon, who was squashed against one of the poles that ran from floor to ceiling – obviously holding it up. The bus was very old – a kind of vintage bus, the like of which Ethan had never seen before. The ceiling was of a pressed metal, with an intricate design – like he'd seen in some of the oldest houses in Melbourne. It was in fantastic condition. Around where the driver sat, all the chrome was polished and the dash was decorated with cards and flowers and beads. A large statue of Jesus took pride of place – there were a lot of Christians in this part of Sumatra.

When they got on, he was sure they'd secured the last three seats. He was wrong. He couldn't believe it as more and more people kept arriving and places were found for them. Seats folded down into the aisle, so that even it was full and the bus was just one mass of bodies pressed together. He hated to think what would happen in an accident; you'd never get out. He'd been fairly relieved when that ride was over and they had been dropped off at the waterfall.

Ethan's glad that this time they get to be on the roof. He's got the wind in his hair, room to stretch out his legs and the most awesome view. Not like Katrin, jammed like a sardine underneath.

As he daydreams, he's really enjoying his smoke. Enjoying it immensely, he thinks, trying out the poshish-sounding word in his mind. It seems to suit. Sitting back, on top of the world, savouring the flavour. Savouring the moment. He's smoked lots of ordinary smokes at home, but there's something special about these. For a start, he actually likes them, whereas the normal ones back home taste kind of… Well, if he's honest, they taste kind of crap. He only does it for something to do. Now, though, he lets the smoke waft around the inside of his mouth, relishing its taste. It is really sweet, but there's a strong peppermint flavour too. That's from the cloves, which tend to pop and crack now and then as they burn. The whole effect is a bit like a menthol, but much, much nicer.

Before he goes home he's going to buy a carton and sneak them in his backpack. It's hard to believe a cigarette could actually feel refreshing, but these do. Like having a cool glass of water, but one that leaves a sticky sweet taste on your lips. And they burn for about ten minutes. The first few he's had to put out because he got sick of them, but now he's used to it. And they're so cheap. From what he can tell, they're about a dollar a packet. No wonder every boy his age and older and all the men seem to smoke here.

As the bus swerves sickeningly to avoid a truck on the wrong side of the road, Ethan slides across the top, using his feet against some sacks of rice to avoid spilling off the side. His heart gives a momentary jump – that's adrenalin, he knows the feeling and its name. But he likes the danger. It's kind of like skating. That moment when you sail right out of the bowl, hang for a sec with the board sticking to your feet like magic. When you have that moment of doubt that you can pull it off.

He casts an eye at Jon. He's seen Ethan's near miss, and he grimaces, then they both laugh. Apart from his white knuckles gripping the steel bars, Jon seems pretty happy. He seems to have shed his fan club too. Ethan thought Jon was going to flip when all those blokes started snuggling up to him. It's so funny. Now he's sitting back looking very relaxed. More relaxed than he's ever seen him, maybe.

Ethan taps the man sitting next to him on the shoulder. "*Rokok?*" he says.

The man holds out his packet of smokes. Ethan takes one and gives the man a crumpled thousand rupiah note. The man smiles and lights the smoke for him, shielding it from the wind. Ethan takes a deep drag.

Jon scrambles over to sit next to him. "Check out that village," he says.

Over the tree tops they can see the pitched roofs of a traditional Karo village, then behind it a cliff with green rice fields. There's a farmer with a water buffalo in harness and they're hand-ploughing the field, calf deep in mud. Behind them is the top of the volcano they're going to climb tomorrow, with its classic cone shape and puffs of smoke popping out, as if for the postcard.

"What a view," says Jon. "Glad I'm not a girl."

"Poor Katrin," Ethan says, laughing.

Ethan's not sure if the waterfall they saw was worth the effort. They'd only stayed about twenty minutes and he's seen a lot better in Australia. But as the bus rolls safely into Berstagi and he clambers down from the roof, he's feeling pretty satisfied with how things are going.

Except he'd love a pizza. Or a nice crusty sausage roll with sauce. Not much chance of that around here, he's thinking.

9

Gunung Sibayak

It's not everyday in your life that you climb a volcano, so at breakfast Ethan is pretty excited. He's eating a potato omelette which is very oily and very delicious and he's drinking his second Coke.

"God! Coke for breakfast! Ethan, that is disgusting!" says Katrin.

"So is thick black coffee with condensed milk and ice cubes."

"It's iced coffee!"

"It looks like shit."

"Try it?"

"Yuk!"

The guest house owner comes over to the table. He's German or Dutch or something and he and Katrin chat in English then in some other language, then back to English. Ethan finds this amazing. He'd thought swapping from one language to another would be more complicated: like using a radio: "Now switching to frequency X. over and out". But it's nothing like that. Sometimes one speaks in English then the other replies in something else. Sometimes the sentences seem to be in English then swap halfway through. But as they go on, they seem to settle into English and before long Ethan's following a lot of it.

The guest house owner lives here and he's married to an Indonesian lady who seems to be a pretty good cook, or so he keeps saying.

Jon has ducked out to get some food for the trek. Last night, when they got back, they went out and got a Padang meal and Jon was so impressed he wants more.

There's a few of the Padang restaurants in Berstagi and they aren't hard to spot. In the window there are shelves and on the shelves are various dishes in large plastic bowls. Inside are rows of tables with little plastic stools gathered around them.

Jon had heard all about Padang food at school, but never tried it. It came from the town of Padang in Sumatra, but was enormously popular with Indonesians and could be found all over the country. The basic idea was that the shop cooked a range of different dishes each day: everything from curried meats, to vegetables, to deep-fried whole fish.

When you sit down, the shop brings over little saucers of the different types of food. One saucer might hold a plate of greens, like spinach or beans cooked with chilli and fish sauce. Another might have a fleshy fillet of some kind of large fish (*ikan*), curried perhaps with coconut. Another might have a crunchy deep-fried little fish. One might be vegetables. There might be several stewed meat dishes – anything from goat (*kambing*), buffalo (*kerbau*), cow (*sapi*), chicken (*ayam*) and, in the non-Muslim areas, pig (*babi*). And all parts of the animal could turn up on your plate. Last night Jon had been pleased he'd asked, so he hadn't gone down the goat stomach (*perut kambing*) path. It certainly looked tasty enough, sitting there in its little orange saucer.

Usually the food is cold, from sitting in the window, which puts a lot of travellers right off. All the guide books warn you to only eat freshly cooked food, to be sure all the germs are dead. Even worse, the food you've been served might have been on ten other tables that day. It is brought out in small portions on saucers. But you only pay for saucers you actually try. Any left untouched are taken away and poured back into the original bowls in the front of the shop and served again later to other customers. There's a lot of good reasons for Westerners to steer clear of Padang food, but mostly it should be OK. Mostly. And it tastes delicious.

Today they're going on a long trek, and Jon is going to ask for three Padang meals *bungkus*. *Bungkus* means "parcel" and is the equivalent of asking for take away. Because they'll be wandering about with food in their packs for several hours, he asks only for *sayur-sayuran dan nasi* (vegetables and rice) which is less likely than meat to go off.

Katrin feels pretty confident she has got the directions to this volcano sorted. Unfortunately, although yesterday they could see it standing with its classic volcano shape on the edge of town, puffing smoke like a cartoon volcano, today the clouds have come in and you can barely see thirty metres across the street. But Roger at the Elshaddai had given her a fairly decent map and she thinks she knows what she's doing.

It's raining already! Just a light sprinkle, hopefully it won't last. But the boys still seem pretty enthusiastic and Katrin doesn't care. Or she doesn't care yet. They haven't started the climb and it's still vaguely warm and humid. Further up the volcano it could get cold and Roger has warned them to take warm clothes and a raincoat.

It's about a ten-minute walk out of town to where the climb starts and it rains gently all the way. Just getting to the edge of town the wind picks up sharply. Katrin pulls out a scarf and winds it around her head to protect her ears.

Signs show them they are entering the reserve for Gunung Sibayak and that it is 2,094 metres high. They stop to read a warning sign in English listing the names of Westerners who have disappeared without trace climbing this volcano. Stick to the paths at all costs, seems to be the message. Katrin isn't worried. She's not taking any risks. She's seen volcanoes before, with their cliffs and steaming hot vents. She's got a pretty good appreciation for the quick death that awaits anyone who does something stupid.

She thinks the boys will be fine. Jon has a very level head. Since their chat the other day, he's seemed much happier – both with her and with Ethan.

Ethan she's not so sure about. He's just a kid, really. He thought the warning sign was amazing, stopping to photograph it. He's obviously impressed by danger – but that doesn't necessarily translate to his being careful. She's met lots of adrenalin junkies – to use Martin's phrase – travelling about. Hooked on danger. Chasing thrills. Seeking out real risks.

She watches Jon now as he strides out in front, his long brown legs propelling him effortlessly up the road. He really is very beautiful. She really loves his eyes; dark like an Indonesian. He talked a little last night after Ethan went to bed.

"How long was your mother ill" she'd asked.

"Which illness?"

It'd been a rhetorical question and she'd smiled a little to acknowledge that she got what he was saying.

"The alcoholism? All my life. The cancer was there for about two years. Or at least it was two years we knew about it. Breast cancer. Then lots of other cancers, as if breast wasn't enough. She spent the last three months in a hospice. I couldn't look after her at home."

"But you looked after Ethan."

"That's right. I was in university by then and had a part-time job." He shrugged his shoulders. "We managed."

Then he'd changed the topic again, before she could ask him more. He wanted to know about her course. Was it really OK for her to defer a medical degree – could she really do that? Why medicine? She'd felt embarrassed to tell him that she wasn't sure. She'd applied and got in and it pleased her family, but she wasn't sure she wanted to be a doctor. She'd felt embarrassed also, telling him about her family. Her mother a university lecturer in chemistry and her father an accountant. A happy marriage. A happy childhood. An older brother and a younger sister, both doing well. No dramas to speak of. It all seemed – well, not boring, just maybe… She couldn't quite put her finger on it… She just didn't think Jon would want to share his story with someone whose life had been so…so easy…

Funny. Since they talked the other night he'd been so friendly and warm. Yet on another level he seemed more distant. He had an extra glass of beer last night and she had deliberately met his eye when she said she was off to bed. But he'd looked away and made a joke about getting a hot shower while they lasted.

Ethan's room was all dark when she went upstairs, but she kept her light on until she heard Jon returning from the bathroom. He walked right by her door, unlocked his and went inside. The walls were so thin she could hear him moving about, undressing and then the loud snap as he turned out the light.

He's not getting my message, she had thought as she snapped her own light off and crawled into bed.

But what message is that? Katrin isn't sure. She thinks she wants Jon to like her. At least it doesn't feel great that he doesn't seem interested. But that's not enough, really, is it?

It's good to have something to think about as they make this climb, because it's pretty tedious and strenuous. And the fog has come in tightly, so even though they've climbed several hundred metres, there's nothing to look at except the black bitumen underfoot and some bare earth and rocks beside the roadway.

It's a bit of a let down, really. Underfoot, it's just a regular road. Except extremely steep, so steep you'd think you'd need a four-wheel drive for some bits. It almost makes Katrin's calves scream.

It's hard to see anyone getting lost here, she thinks. A heart attack maybe.

Jon's obviously not concerned about safety. He's got out way ahead. That's like him, she thinks. He's not enjoying this, so he digs deep to try and get it over with as soon as he can.

By contrast, Ethan's fallen back a little and Katrin is content not to push herself. Rounding a bend there's a suitable sized rock to sit on and she plants herself to wait for Ethan.

She's fairly fit, so by the time he gets to her a minute or two later her breathing is back to normal.

He's gasping. "Fucking hell!" he mutters.

"Too many of those kretek cigarettes," says Katrin.

"Speaking of which." His breathing has settled quickly and he pulls a near full packet of Garams from his pocket.

"God, I'm not waiting for you to smoke that."

"I got a half one I started before."

"You're going to smoke a butt?" She doesn't try to hide her disgust.

"It's not a butt. I broke it off clean. It's like a mini smoke."

"Oh, nice," says Katrin, piling on the sarcasm. "I'm off. Don't be too long."

Jon's stopped where the road ends and the footpath begins. It's pretty clearly marked, at least here, but he has no doubt that things will get more difficult. You don't get large numbers of trekkers getting lost and just never being found, ever, unless the terrain is pretty dangerous.

While he waits he pulls out a packet of the nasty Indonesian biscuits he bought this morning. They seem to be an imitation of Oreos, but they're not very nice. Still he woofs down about six and drinks half a litre of water.

Katrin comes along next, puffing respectably, followed by Ethan, who looks really buggered. Jon shares out some biscuits and waits with them while they catch their breath and have a drink.

All the while it's raining steadily. Not the tropical downpour of Bukit Lawang. More like a Melbourne winter, grey, gloomy skies, persistent drizzle and wind.

And the fog doesn't look like lifting.

Still they set off down the footpath, which has been concreted. It's not as steep as the road, except in places. The climb is more gradual and it's easier for the group to stay together.

"I smell sulphur," says Katrin.

"Smells like fucking rotten eggs," says Ethan.

"Doesn't it!" Jon feels like he's going to gag.

"Volcanoes all seem to smell like this. We must be getting closer to the top."

"Not that you'd know. Fuck, this fog is thick!" Ethan's language is deteriorating as he's getting tired. Every second word now seems to be fuck.

But he has a point. When Jon looks down at his feet he can see the faint swirl of mist. As he scans along the track, it's almost completely obliterated within three of four metres.

Still it's safe enough. It's a concrete footpath! How anyone could get lost here is a mystery.

"I need a piss," says Ethan.

Jon swings around "What's stopping you."

"Go up ahead and wait for me. Don't turn round."

Jon's seen Ethan piss a million times; it's Katrin who's provoked Ethan's sudden shyness. Jon shrugs and gives Katrin a smile as they move along a little.

It takes only seconds, but it's as though Ethan has completely disappeared into the whiteness. It seems to shut out noise too. Though he couldn't be more than twenty metres away, Jon and Katrin's world is totally silent, bar the sound of the breeze.

"I need to go too," says Katrin.

"Want me to walk on ahead?"

"He'll catch me up. Boys are always faster."

"Let's wait for him then. Then Ethan and I will go on ahead and give you some privacy."

She laughs. "It's not so easy for a girl. I don't want to squat here on the concrete." She knows she's being silly and is laughing at herself. Suddenly she reminds him of a cat, searching for the perfect spot.

"I wouldn't step off the path. For all we know there might be a cliff only metres away."

They hear Ethan's footsteps on the concrete, a second or two before they see him. It is weird, almost ghostly. His footsteps seem to echo in the whiteness. Jon's never been to London, but this reminds him of the creepy London fog in Jack the Ripper films he's seen. It's got a coldness – an icy dampness – about it too. You'd never believe you were almost at the equator.

"Bloody hell. Couldn't even see where my piss ended up," says Ethan. "This is pretty freaky."

The fog has an eerie white brightness about it. It almost hurts the eyes. And it's closing in, visibly, as they stand there.

"Now I see what might have happened to those people. If you left the path here, you'd never find your way back."

Katrin has unconsciously moved closer to Jon.

He looks down, but now he can only barely make out their feet. This is visibility of about a metre.

"You'd have to be dumb to do that in these conditions," says Ethan.

"But ten minutes ago we had visibility of twenty-five to thirty metres. You'd have thought nothing of ducking off down some dirt path to check out something."

"Do you think that's what happened?" says Katrin.

"Maybe. I saw some old paths earlier. Perhaps they saw an animal or a bird."

"Or some guy needing a shit, or something," says Ethan.

His crudity seems unnecessary and Jon is irritated.

"You two go on a little. I must make my own *kamar kecil*," says Katrin. "But wait for me. Just go a little way."

Jon shuffles off first, with Ethan very close behind. He's moving very slowly. He can see the path, but only a step or so in front of him. Then suddenly it stops and he sees only orange clay soil. He stops suddenly and Ethan bumps gently into him.

"What's up?"

"The path's gone."

"How can it be gone?"

"Buggered if I know," says Jon. "It just stops."

Ethan comes to stand beside him. They squat down to be sure, but Jon is right. The last square of concrete just stops. It's joined to the path they came up on one side, but its three other sides end in dirt.

"Now what?" says Ethan.

"Search me." Jon's a bit sick of having to be in charge. "Maybe I'll walk on a bit and see what's there." Now he's being deliberately reckless, just to see if Ethan will notice.

But Ethan isn't biting. "That rotten egg smell is really strong. I reckon this must be near the top," he says, ignoring Jon's really stupid idea. "I reckon we wait it out here for a while."

"Well, we'll wait for Katrin, anyway."

She isn't far away, which suits Ethan because it's just started drizzling.

"This is quite awful," she says as she appears out of the fog. She looks a little relieved to find Jon and Ethan, though they couldn't have been more than twenty or thirty metres away.

"So what now?" says Ethan.

"It's a pity to go back. I think we must be almost on top."

"I'm not sure it's that safe either," says Jon. "Not until the fog lifts a little."

"Meanwhile, it starts to rain."

"We can build a bush hut," says Jon pointing to the undergrowth.

Ethan rolls his eyes. Jon wouldn't know the first thing about bush skills.

"Burrow in, you mean? Like rabbits?" This amuses Katrin.

"Yeah, exactly." He lifts up the branches of one bush and sure enough the ground is dry underneath. "Try it?" he says to Katrin.

"Sure. Why not?" she says and crawls under.

"Ethan?"

He looks dubious. "You first."

Jon squeezes in and sure enough the branches give way to create a snug dry space. He pushes further, so there will be room for Ethan. "Come on. You'll get cold out there."

Ethan scrambles in and, sure enough, he feels immediately warmer out of the weather. "We could sleep here," he says.

"God, I hope not!" Katrin snorts.

"We might have too if that fog gets worse."

Katrin obviously thinks this is ridiculous. "Worse? How could it get worse!"

"Well, right now you can see your feet. Imagine trying to follow that path if visibility stops at your waist or knees."

"You could crawl down," Ethan suggests.

It's a stupid idea and Jon and Katrin ignore it.

"I can't believe it can get worse. This is the tropics! Even in Belgium we do not have fog so bad that you cannot see your own feet."

Jon's not going to argue. Maybe she's right, maybe she's wrong. But he's got a bit of an inkling of what might have gone wrong to have so many people die up here.

"Well, we gotta pass some time now. Any suggestions."

"We could play I spy," offers Ethan. Jon laughs and kicks him in the thigh.

"What is I spy?" says Katrin.

"You know, 'I spy something beginning with…F.' Something that can be seen from where you are. And you have to guess."

"But we can't see anything!"

Ethan groans. "Der! That's the joke. I spy something beginning with F – fog!"

Katrin chuckles. "Funny. But we can still play, I think. It will just be more challenging."

"How – you going to speak Belgian?" asks Ethan.

"Ethan, I have already told you. In Belgium we speak French or Flemish. There is no such thing as Belgian. But to answer your question. Yes, we can use English. I will start, OK?"

"OK."

Katrin looks around in thought. "I spy something beginning with…H."

"Hill, hat, heather, heath," says Jon.

"Who the fuck are Heather and Heath?" says Ethan.

"There's no need to say 'fuck' every second word," says Jon.

"Chill, bro! How about hand?"

"No."

"Hair?" says Jon.

"No."

"Handsome?"

"Who? You or Ethan?" laughs Katrin. "But that is an adjective. It must be a noun, yes?"

Ethan's frustrated already. "This is English?"

"Of course."

Jon and Ethan look at each other. They've got no idea.

"What is it?" says Ethan at last.

"That means I get to choose another – until you can guess?"

"Yeah. That's the rule."

She waits until Jon nods his agreement. "Human."

As the game goes on Ethan gets bored. He's never going to get any of these words. E for epidermis (medical terms were banned after that). C for confidant (there was a debate over whether that was an adjective, but Katrin said it with an accent and said it was someone you confide in. Jon knew that word, but he tried to argue it was French). G for guardian. S for sibling (Jon was pissed he didn't get that one straight after guardian).

Ethan knows Jon's not enjoying this much, but he's a patient bastard. He'll hang in there and take his flogging, because he's already thought up a dozen words that Katrin won't guess. He just needs to get one of hers.

They're still at it a few minutes later and Ethan crawls to the opening of their shelter. The fog is still as thick as before, but it seems like the drizzle has stopped.

Just then there are footsteps. He hears them just a second before a pair of blue jeans appear in front of his face.

Blue Jeans stops and turns backward to speak to a second set of footsteps that are still hidden in fog.

Ethan lies in wait. He can't resist the opportunity. "What's up?" he barks suddenly, maximising the surprise.

Blue Jeans jumps about a foot in the air. There is a kind of strangled man-gasp and hiking boots take a hurried step backwards, slipping a little and almost losing balance. Composing himself, Blue Jeans bends at the waist to poke his head down and check out the source of the noise. The face appears right in front of Ethan, so close he can feel the man's breath. He is one of those very blond European types. Ethan's seen him before, back in Medan. His girlfriend – equally blonde – is right behind him.

Ethan laughs. "Hi, there," he says.

"Hel-lo," says Blue Jeans. "What are you doing in the tree?" The accent is a thick German one. His "what" sounds like "vot" and his "the" is a harsh sounding "zee".

Ethan scrambles out. "Keeping warm," he says. "Can't see a bloody thing in this fog."

Jon and Katrin are rattling around in the bushes and soon they stumble awkwardly out.

Jon looks embarrassed, as if he's been caught doing something really stupid. "Hi, there," he says. "You two are brave walking about in this fog."

"It is better now, I think," says Blue Jeans.

And he's right. Visibility is still pretty ordinary but the five of them can all see each other easily enough and the path now stretches up the slope a few metres before disappearing again.

"This wind is stronger now," says Katrin. "Maybe it will blow the fog away."

Ethan thinks this sounds ridiculous and he's about to scoff at the idea, when there's an extra forceful burst of air. For a moment they turn their backs to it, but it only lasts a second and the fog lifts off. It's a magic moment; there's even a beam of sunlight. Ahead, the path is clear for a hundred metres or so.

"We must ascend to the top now, I think," says Blue Jeans, "while there is this break in the weather." For a second Ethan is caught up in the moment. He feels a burst of adrenalin. Then it's gone and he wants to giggle. This whole scene reminds him of climbers making their assaults on Everest.

But still he makes sure he's in front, ducking around Katrin and Jon to lead off. Ahead, the fog is lifting off even further. He can now see the whole top of the volcano. They were really close, less than a hundred metres from the highest point. But it isn't like he'd imagined. From a distance the volcanos around here had looked pointy, like a classic volcano shape. Up here it's flat. There's no crater to speak of, just a dip with steam coming out of it. Everywhere there are rocks – most of them a whitish colour. It's actually fairly ugly and boring, like a quarry. And although the fog has lifted so he can see it, it hasn't lifted enough to see any kind of view. He doesn't even bother getting his camera out.

Blue Jeans and his girlfriend, though, they've whipped a tripod out of their backpack and Blue Jeans is snapping away on a pretty nifty looking camera – one of those digital ones that still do all the manual stuff that real photographers like to do.

As they start snapping away, Ethan picks up a rock and lobs it into the crater.

"Be careful," says Katrin. "Maybe you'll cause the eruption."

She's joking. Ethan thinks she's poking a bit of fun at Blue Jeans' seriousness and the whole anti-climactic feeling of this adventure, so he laughs.

"This place really stinks," he says and lobs just one last stone. "I'm gunna start going down."

"We should go together, I think. I don't think they'll be long."

They've moved the tripod around a bit and are snapping away from a different angle. Both of them stand behind the camera. Blue Jeans is doing the shooting and Girlfriend is making suggestions in their language. It strikes Ethan that their photo album will be pretty dull. Shots of rocks. He thinks it's pretty telling that neither of them has moved in front of the camera.

"Hey, Ethan!"

He hears Jon calling him and turns round.

Jon has his camera out. "I'll get Katrin to get a shot of us on top of our first volcano."

Ethan's embarrassed "Nah, I'll take it. Katrin and you can be in it."

"But it's not my first volcano," she protests.

"Come on," says Jon and before he can move away, Jon wraps his long arms around him from behind. He's bloody strong and quickly he's tipped Ethan backwards and off balance so his weight rests against his brother's chest. Ethan struggles and throws an elbow back, but Jon only grips him harder. He starts to drag him backwards away from Katrin. Ethan tries to hold his ground, but his heels just scrape against the dirt cutting two lines, like when a body has been dragged on TV.

"Quick," shouts Jon, his breath warm next to his ear. "Take it before he escapes."

10

Elshadai Guest House, Berstagi

In the end, Katrin took about six shots before Jon let Ethan spill to the ground. Even Blue Jeans and Girlfriend – whose names were actually Martin and Gretel – had finished with the rocks and taken a couple of shots.

Martin has his camera out now. They're sitting together at a table back at the Elshaddai, where Martin and Gretel are also staying and Martin's showing Ethan the shots he took on Gunung Sibayak. They're actually pretty good, but there are too many of them. They'd used a telephoto lens and taken shots of the crater close up.

The shot of Ethan and Jon is also a good one. They took it after Ethan had recovered from the shock of Jon grabbing him like that, and regained his composure. In it he's laughing and he looks like he's set to punch Jon in the groin. Jon's laughing too, but has spotted the danger and is taking evasive action. Ethan likes it. He's asked Martin for a copy, but because it is an eight point something megapixel, whiz bang camera, the photo files are too big for email so Martin must get it burned to disk.

Jon's there too. Katrin and Gretel are off speaking German together on another table. The men have been left to talk English, which Gretel doesn't like to do. Jon likes Martin's photo too. It's better than the ones Katrin took. Standing behind Ethan he'd missed his brother's facial expressions, but Katrin's camera had frozen them. There had been an angry desperation on Ethan's face that Jon feels deeply uncomfortable with. He'd just been mucking about. But poor Ethan looked really upset.

Martin is the same German traveller that Jon saw at Sugar's guest house back in Medan. Jon's interested to hear how he got on with his trek, so he asks him about it.

"Oh my God! Oh my God! Well, I am not so sure that my guide

was a good one," says Martin. "We were very clear that we wanted to see animals. But, after two days of walking, walking. Nothing! So we say maybe we return to Bukit Lawang and find different guide. That was a mistake!" Martin slaps himself on the forehead dramatically. "Oh, what a mistake!"

"How come?" prompts Ethan.

"Well, by this time we are thinking maybe this guide know not much about the jungle. But he do not wish us to leave him. So he say – we go further into jungle. Further from villages. More animals there, you know."

Ethan and Jon are nodding.

"So another day goes by. Always it is raining. We are pretty angry and tired. Then we come around a corner on the path and there is a man there with a gun."

"Wow" says Ethan.

"Ja – he is standing there waiting for us. He point his gun and is speaking with our guide in Indonesian. Our fucking guide was fucking terrified, y'know."

"Was he a rebel?" asks Jon.

"Well, that is what I was thinking… But…"

"What sort of gun was it," interrupts Ethan.

"Well, I don't know. I'm no expert, but something military – maybe an M16."

"Cool!" says Ethan.

"But you don't think he was a rebel?"

"Our guide he take us away and we walk very fast for about three hours, before he spoke to us at all. We thinking he thinking we is being watched, the whole way."

"Wow," says Ethan.

"Then he say, we must not go that way. I say who is that man? Is he rebel? Guide does not want to talk, but eventually he say that he was not rebel. He was logger. Someone taking logs illegally from the jungle."

"I've heard that's a big problem."

"Ja, big problem. Guide he say that logger make big problem in forest. He say they take hundreds of trees and move them down the river, by – how you say…" Martin struggles for the English word."

"They float them?"

"Ja, ja. Float. That is what he say. The loggers, they build a dam and store the logs, then when they are ready, they float the logs to a place where they have trucks waiting to remove them."

"Hey, Jon, what about those logs we saw on the river?"

"Yeah, I was just thinking about that."

"We saw some huge trees floating down the river. Jon nearly got killed by one crossing a log bridge."

"And there was that one nearly wiped out the canoe," Jon adds.

"And where was this?"

"At Bukit Lawang," says Jon. "And further upstream on the Bohorok River."

"I think, maybe they are logs that escape from the dam," says Martin.

"You think?"

"Ja, maybe. I think maybe it is good we are away from that place."

Ethan is still awake. He's lying in the dark smoking a cigarette, snuggled up under the covers, only his ciggie hand and face poking out. It's surprisingly cold here.

Beside his bed is a table and on the table is an ashtray and a bottle of the most disgusting whisky he's ever tasted. It's called Mansion House and it has a picture of a big mansion on the label. He finds it weird. Why would you call a brand of whisky Mansion House? The alcohol content is only twenty per cent, too, which is about half that of standard whisky back home. The ingredients – in Indonesian – are pretty scary. Basically it seems to be alcohol mixed with caramel colouring. It's got this really toxic chemically smell. He's mixed it with Coke, but even that still barely made it drinkable.

He'd gone to bed early a couple of hours ago. Katrin, Gretel, Jon and Martin were going to play cards. He'd bought the Coke from the restaurant and wished all good night. Then he slipped out the front door into the main street. There wasn't much open, but he found a little shop. It seemed to sell just about everything, from cans of food, to soft drinks, newspapers, fruit, pots and pans and lots of plastic junk. No one was about except for an old man sleeping on a bench.

He stood there for a moment or two, then woke the old man up. "*Rokok*," he said, making the motion of smoking. "*Satu paket. Garam.*"

The old man understood and got him a packet of clove cigarettes.

"*Harga?*" asked Ethan and the man held up seven fingers to indicate seven thousand rupiah. Ethan dug some scruffy notes out of his pocket. "Whisky?" he asked, making the motion of drinking.

The old man seemed to understand but frowned and shook his head, averting his eyes. He was wearing that little Muslim cap, the *peci* – probably the wrong person to ask, Ethan thought.

Outside the shop he'd lit a cigarette and surveyed the street. Most shops were closed and he honestly couldn't remember seeing a shop that sold alcohol all day. The restaurant in the guest house had it for tourists, but he hadn't wanted to buy it in front of Jon. Wandering along a little, he saw some young guys crowded about, all smoking and talking. They just looked to him like a bunch of guys back home, bored and possibly up to no good. He subtly wandered in their direction, but hung back a little.

One peeled off to leave, waving goodbye to the others. He was walking in Ethan's direction and just as he reached him, Ethan said, "Excuse me. Do you speak English?"

He stopped and grinned at Ethan. "Yes, a little," he said.

"I want to buy some drink, some whisky." Ethan made the motion of drinking.

The guy had looked confused.

"Whisky," Ethan said again. He made the motion of unscrewing a cap and pouring a glass.

"Ah, Mansion House!" said the guy.

Ethan had no idea what that was, but the look of recognition on the fellow's face was unmistakable.

"You can get?"

He nodded.

"*Harga?*" He could see the guy adding his cut to the normal price.

"*Lima puluh,*" he said. The words mean "fifty", but Ethan knew he meant fifty thousand. It's less than ten dollars, but it's still a rip off.

"*Mahal!*" he said.

The guy shrugged and Ethan knew he was being an idiot. The poor kid didn't approach him, after all. "OK, OK!" he agreed. He was feeling like a cheap bastard denying this bloke a dollar or two, when it was nothing to him. He still had the equivalent of twenty dollars left over from the fifty Jon let him have back in Malaysia – things are so incredibly cheap here. So, trying to smooth things over he started smiling and saying, "*Bagus! Bagus! Terima kasih!*" to show he was happy and grateful.

To Ethan's astonishment, the guy took his hand and led him off down a side street. He felt a stab of nervousness. Am I about to be mugged, he'd thought? But he went anyway, putting one foot in front of another until he was standing holding hands with his new friend down a very dark lane way. They stopped and he could see the glow of the guy's smoke as he raised it to his lips. Ethan was nervous as hell by then and too shocked even to pull his hand away.

The guy gave his hand a squeeze and dropped it. He slapped Ethan's shoulder. "Wait here," he said.

Ethan's eyes had adjusted to the blackness and he was able to make out the shadowy form of the guy as he knocked on a wooden window shutter. It opened quickly, spilling yellow light from an oil lamp out into the street. Ethan's eyes made another adjustment and he could see the face of a wizened old Chinese man, his long stringy beard hanging down his chest. The transaction took only seconds – Ethan couldn't see exactly what his friend paid for the bottle, but he didn't care. The window was snapped shut without a word and the bottle was in his palm in seconds.

Now he's made himself drink most of it, despite the taste. He's feeling pretty happy and relaxed. He hears the clump of footsteps outside and the voices of Martin and Gretel as they chat in German then take turns using the bathroom. Jon and Katrin are still downstairs and Ethan realises he is unconsciously waiting for them.

He forces down another glass of the syrupy alcoholic Coke and lights another cigarette. He lies there puffing away in the dark, watching the chinks of light around the door frame.

They are down there alone a long time and Ethan decides to go to sleep. He gets up, uses the toilet, brushes his teeth. Then back in bed he pulls the pillow over his head. It doesn't work. Twenty minutes later he's still awake.

Eventually he hears more footsteps. It must be Jon and Katrin, but they don't say a word. Two sets of feet cross the lino outside his door and pass by Jon's room. Further down the hall he hears a key in a lock and whispers, then a door shutting. He pulls the pillow tighter around his head.

11

Somewhere near Pematangsiantar

This is not how Katrin thought she'd be spending "the morning after" with Jon. The three of them are sitting on bench seats in a stationary bemo. It's parked in a dusty yard large enough for a dozen vehicles, but it's empty apart from them. No one is about apart from the driver.

This bemo doesn't have a departure time. The driver won't move until enough passengers arrive. He doesn't know when that'll be and from the way he's now sleeping across the yard under that tree, he's not expecting a ten o'clock rush.

It's been half an hour already. And what's worse, for what seems like about the last ten minutes, they've been listening to the most blood-curdling terrified cries of a pig being slaughtered somewhere close by. It's awful. You can't just ignore it and carry on chatting. So the whole time they've been sitting in silence listening, eyes on the floor, waiting and hoping for it to be over.

Katrin will never eat pork again – maybe never even eat again. She wonders why it's taking so long.

It's been a bad morning for Katrin. It's hard to describe how devastated she's feeling. She is utterly flat and unable to raise any kind of enthusiasm. This was always going to be a long and boring transport day. An awkward journey involving three different buses, to the town of Parapat on the banks of Lake Toba, and then a ferry ride over to the island in the middle of the lake.

But they overrode the first bus and didn't get out where they should have. Then Jon got some pretty poor advice about what to do next, listening to some random man who told them to get in a bemo. No sooner were they in it than it shot off down some gravelly track that was somehow meant to be taking them closer to Pematangsiantar, the big town where the proper buses stop.

Funny things happen to you when you're travelling. You find yourself being taken somewhere and you know it's almost certainly a mistake, but you just sit there and let it happen. But it was hard to know what else to do. The three of them were sitting in the back, the driver in the front.

She's not sure whether the bemo ride was a rip off – it cost a ridiculous hundred thousand rupiah, but it's a bit hard to complain. They'd been stupid and not fixed a price first. But then it dropped them here, which is not where they wanted to be. They might be closer to Pematangsiantar, but that isn't going to help if they stay stranded in this obscure little town that isn't even marked in the Lonely Planet.

How long do we just sit here? And how long does it take to kill a poor defenceless creature, for fuck's sake!

And if that's not enough, this whole thing with Jon seems to have gone – how do these Australians say? Pear shaped.

She sneaks a look across at him now. He's all hunched up, his long body bent unnaturally to fit under the low roof of the bemo. He looks tense and anxious and he doesn't look like he's ever going to meet her gaze again.

Ethan is sitting as far away from both of them as he can. He has vomited three times in public this morning. He reeks of alcohol. It seems to be coming out the pores of his skin. He's sweaty, his hair greasy. He is dreadfully pale. If only he could stand outside himself and see how he looks. It's sad. And today Jon doesn't seem up to dealing with it. He's barely spoken to Ethan either.

Katrin has been mulling over this situation with Jon for days now. She knows she likes him, but how much and in exactly what way, she hasn't been entirely sure.

Well, that's not exactly true. There is a physical attraction. And there is a great basis for friendship – but sometimes that's the problem. Last night she'd been turning it over and over in her mind. If she were to move the relationship in a physical direction, and decided it was a mistake, there'd be no going back. More than likely she'd lose Jon's friendship.

So she'd tried to have it both ways. In some crazy moment after Gretel and Martin went to bed, she thought she could somehow orchestrate this thing with Jon so she could – another English phrase she likes – "have her cake and eat it too".

Right now Katrin is frowning at the memory. She sneaks another look at him. His eyes haven't moved. They're still locked on the floor and he's making swirls in the dust with the edge of his thong. He's wearing long pants, but Katrin can see the lean line of calf extending upwards inside the cuff. His skin looks warm and his body hard and strong, his biceps clearly visible under his T-shirt. She pushes the memory of his arms around her away. It's tinged now with embarrassment, and she cringes when she thinks of it.

He hasn't shaved today and there is a fine black stubble on his jaw and lip. Somehow it makes him look more Indonesian.

Sometimes the desire to touch Jon burns in her stomach like a hunger. She can resist it but, like hunger, it's uncomfortable and difficult to ignore. And something about him also scares her. There is a big part of Jon that he protects and keeps to himself. To fall in love with him, she'd have to get to see that side – but until she's seen it, how does she know if she'll love it or be repulsed by it?

How nice it would be to be able to "try and not buy", to explore the physical side but be able to take a step back afterwards and have it not have changed anything.

So last night she kind of steered the conversation around until somehow they'd decided that it would be OK for them to sleep together as long as it was just as friends. You know – no kissing, no touching in the wrong places and definitely no sex.

Honestly, you would have thought from how stupid they were that they were both drunk – but, no, they'd had only a couple of glasses of the local *arak*. But then it was home-made – arriving in an old Coke bottle with a cork shoved into it. A boy of about twelve came in asking for Martin, who ducked outside like he was buying drugs and returned with it in a plastic bag.

Who knows how strong it actually was. It tasted a lot like you'd imagine turpentine to taste, but with Coke added it wasn't bad. Ethan had gone to bed early and Jon seemed relieved to have him gone. Even before the arak arrived, he'd loosened up a lot.

Come to think of it, they'd finished that Coke bottle of arak between the four of them, Jon and Katrin having the last third together after Martin and Gretel went to bed.

"So," she'd said, "I think it is such a shame that friendships between men and women are complicated by sex." It was that kind of mushy drunken conversation. On and on she went, or so it seems now. And she meant it, at the time. It really had seemed like a good idea.

Well, that lasted all of about five minutes once they were in bed together. Suddenly she was kissing him and he had rolled so that he was lying half on top of her, his body warm along the length of hers.

She raises her hand to her face as she thinks of it. Flashbacks can be a terrible thing. She knew she'd been more than into it. She remembers moaning, her breath coming quickly.

Then he lifted himself up and she opened her eyes to look at him. He'd looked weird, kind of freaked out.

"I'm sorry," he'd said. Then he was up and sitting on the edge of the bed. "I can't."

"It's OK," she'd said. But it wasn't. Her face burned with shame. Thank God she was still dressed.

"It's not you," offered Jon.

Katrin hadn't got it at all. Was he saying he wasn't interested? Or was it just that he wasn't interested right then? Was he feeling sick from the arak? Did he not fancy her? Was there something physical about her that had put him off? She had so many questions but she was too embarrassed to ask them. Saying as little as possible seemed like the coolest possible move under the circumstances.

"Hey, we're friends – right?" she said. Her tone was light, unconcerned.

"Yeah, sure." Jon gave her a weak smile. "I'm really sorry. This is awful." Suddenly he had looked very young and sad.

"You want to hop back into bed? We'll just sleep. Like we said." As soon as she'd said it she'd wished she hadn't. She'd felt sorry for him and sorry for herself. For a second she'd hoped that they could comfort each other. But it had just opened the door to a second rejection.

"I can't. I'm sorry. I think it's best if I go back to my own room now." And he'd slipped his shoes back on and grabbed his jacket.

Then there was a moment of hesitation when Katrin could see him wondering whether he was supposed to kiss her goodbye now. You'd kiss someone goodbye if you'd just had a one-night stand, but what was this?

He'd made a jerky movement towards her and she pulled back without meaning to. They'd both laughed. He'd tried again and this time he kissed her cheek lightly.

"I'll talk to you tomorrow," he'd said as he was leaving.

But he hadn't.

She'd lain awake for most of the night, feeling hurt and embarrassed and anxious about how things would go the next day. She eventually dozed off and when she awoke, it was morning.

Jon wasn't in his room – or he wasn't answering – when she tapped on the door.

Passing the bathroom, she'd heard vomiting noises. She knocked and called softly, "Are you OK?" She heard coughing sounds – an attempt to disguise what was really going on in there.

Whoever it was didn't answer, but from the sounds of movement, they weren't dying so she left. Downstairs Gretel and Martin were eating banana pancakes and drinking thick sugary coffee. Ethan was nowhere to be seen.

Because the Australians weren't there Katrin, Martin and Gretel chatted in German, an inane breakfast conversation going over the night before. After a while Ethan had come down looking as hung over as can be. He ordered Coke and fried eggs and fried potatoes and a pancake and when it arrived he stared at it for a minute of two, before making a mad rush for the bathroom.

Jon had arrived about this time, and Martin made a big deal about telling him that his younger brother – who had gone to bed sober – was now suffering the effects of a massive hangover. He wasn't very subtle and Jon looked stressed by the whole thing.

Jon's eyes met hers when he said "Hi" but they had shot away immediately, so Katrin was feeling pretty awkward and impatient to have things sorted out.

But it'd been impossible to get him alone. There'd been a few words exchanged about getting on the right bus and what to do when they got off at the wrong place, but nothing meaningful had been spoken in the two hours they'd spent together this morning.

She had thought a lot of things might happen if she got together with Jon. But this wasn't one of them.

At last that poor animal is dead.

Jon sucks in a deep breath and settles further back into the bench seat. He's relieved. That noise was freaking him out. People often say stuff like "I thought I was going to be sick" when something brutal or violent happens or someone is badly hurt. It's their way of trying to get across how shocking it is to feel that bad about something that is happening to someone else – or, in this case, to an animal. And saying you're going to physically chuck up – an involuntary violent spasm that racks your body – kind of gets across the power of the emotion.

But he thinks it's rubbish really. Sure, if he found a body and it really stunk, vomiting might follow as an involuntary physical reaction, to a chemical catalyst – a noxious smell. There's an evolutionary reason for that. Rotting carcasses pose a health risk – just look at how dead carcasses cause cholera and other diseases. Being repelled by them is good for survival. The more put off you are by them, the less chance you've got of catching something fatal.

But for thoughts in his mind to cause his body to react outside his control and actually vomit, that seems kind of odd to him. He can't get his head around it.

He's been thinking about it while he's been sitting here listening to those awful cries. And then, because it was bothering him so much, he purposefully narrowed his thoughts even further, focusing on the dust on the floor and trying to create a perfect infinity symbol using his thong. He knows the symbol well: it's like an eight, laid on its side – ∞

It was easy enough to trace the first half, but coming back for the second half, he couldn't stop the trailing edge of his thong from collapsing the edges of the first half. Over and over he tried. Eventually the screaming had stopped, just as he was able to tilt his foot at a good enough angle to make the symbol.

Something about the final silence of the pig seems to have set Ethan off again and he's scrambled out of the bemo and is emptying his stomach. Funny, Jon's thinking. You'd think evolution would have slowly wiped out drunkenness. But then again, maybe it's drunken moments that get people into bed together, causing babies to be born in the first place.

But he can hardly pick on Ethan after his own performance last night.

He wonders about Sharon. His mother and Ethan's. She never liked it when he called her "Mum". Not until she was sick and in the hospital for the last time, then she started trying to get him to say it.

Give Mum a kiss…

He has no idea how long she'd been a drinker – he just knew it had always seemed that way to him.

But what about when she met his father? He was a Christian, so he may have liked a drink. Jon can't see his mother being remotely interested in some teetotaller or a Muslim who didn't drink.

Jon hates the idea that he might be the result of a drunken roll in the sack. You know, where you come from – the mechanics of it – doesn't occur to you until you get to a certain age. It's weird. You're just you and you're just here.

He knew they'd met at Lake Toba twenty years ago – just his age plus nine months. They hadn't been boyfriend-girlfriend, but Sharon said they'd spent a week or so together. His father was a local guy about ten years younger than Sharon and she hadn't even seriously thought about a relationship with him. So she'd left after a while with an address to send a postcard, some photos and the beginnings of Jon growing quietly in her belly.

Darwin. That was his father's name.

"Darwin, like the Australian city," his father had said to Sharon when they met.

Jon had been shocked in high school to find out about Charles Darwin, the famous naturalist who first proposed the theory of evolution back in the nineteenth century.

He'd come home and told Sharon about it and she'd said, "Yeah, that too," but he could tell the connection hadn't occurred to her before.

He wondered if his father knew all about Darwin, or if his father's mother – his grandmother – had just liked the name. Sometimes stuff happens like that.

Sharon and Darwin. Darwin and Sharon. You could just tell from putting those two names together that it would never work. But when she found out she was pregnant, Sharon did try. She returned to Lake Toba and married young Darwin. He'd only been seventeen, but his father agreed and then Sharon took Darwin back to Australia.

She'd never run him down or tried to say he was a bad husband, and Jon is glad about that. It's something positive he can remember his mother for. She'd just said that Darwin was unhappy in Australia because he was away from his home and because he didn't know any other Indonesian people there.

Jon understands – especially now he's seen Sumatra. His father was younger than he is now. A young man from the village, living with an alcoholic and their small child in an Australian city. Jon is surprised he stayed for five years.

He doesn't know for sure, but he suspects it was the arrival of Ethan's father on the scene that finally sent him packing.

Jon actually remembers his father and he knows he loved him. He remembers playing soccer in the park and riding on his father's shoulders.

There were a couple of photographs too – a very young Darwin sunbaking on concrete, bare-chested and wearing only a pair of cut down jeans. That was from Lake Toba, Sharon had said. Darwin holding him at the hospital after he was born. And a birthday photograph from when he was three. But really, it was Jon and Sharon in most of the photos: there are some from his first Christmas, and from a holiday to Rye. And just random photos of Jon, right up to about when he started school. After that there's just the school photos from each year.

He'd never really thought about these two absences much. After all, his dad's absence seemed to fit with him not having a dad. And everyone takes lots of photos of a first baby – poor Ethan has hardly any photos of him except school ones.

But then a thought strikes Jon for the first time. Was it his dad with the camera? Is that why there are all those baby photos of him with his mother? Then none after his father left? And none of baby Ethan?

Jon wishes he had better control of his feelings, because suddenly he's feeling really shattered for the second time in two days.

12

Danau Toba

"**S**ilvan! Hey, Silvan!"

Jon looks up from his book to catch Ethan sprint down the deck waving madly. He brakes sharply at the narrow gangplank. There's an elderly European man, slowly shuffling across.

"Hey, Silvan!" he yells again and vaults the railing. He balances for a moment on the edge of the ferry, then leaps for the wharf, just making it.

"What is the excitement with him?" asks Katrin in her quaintly not-quite-perfect English. She's been dozing in the sun.

They're in Parapat, on the shore of Lake Toba, waiting for the ferry to leave for Samosir Island.

"That guy." Jon indicates over to the wharf.

There are probably fifty people standing around. They're mainly locals, with a handful of tourists.

Katrin's eyes search the crowd. She doesn't know who he means. "Which one?" she asks.

"The one getting out of the bemo. With the hair."

Ethan has reached the bemo and is shaking hands with a surfie-type man, with bleached almost white hair, long board shorts, sandals and a Billabong T-shirt.

"The old man?" says Katrin.

Jon laughs. Silvan would freak. "Yeah. With the surfboard."

Ethan waits while two other backpackers squeeze out the door and packs and surfboards are handed down from the roof. Ethan grabs Silvan's surfboard and skips across the gangplank onto the ferry.

Silvan follows him carrying his pack.

Katrin laughs. "I think maybe someone exaggerated the waves." She indicates the glassy smooth surface of Lake Toba.

"Hey, Jon! Look who's here!"

Jon can't believe how Ethan seems to have shaken that hangover off. You'd never know he was the same sick puppy whose emptied his guts over half of Sumatra today.

"Howdy, Jon," says Silvan, plonking himself down on a bench seat, directly in the sun. His skin is brown and dry, like leather. He looks every bit the authentic drop out surfer from the sixties. "Who's your friend?"

Jon doesn't like the way Silvan's pale blue eyes linger over Katrin, but he's got no real call to be rude, so he extends a hand and a smile. "Gidday, Silvan. Fancy seeing you here," says Jon. "Katrin, this is Silvan."

"The pleasure is mine," Silvan says taking Katrin's fingers in his large palm and curling them around so it's him doing all the shaking. He doesn't quite go so far as to lay a kiss on her hand, but it's that kind of shake.

"And who are your friends, Silvan?" Jon says, indicating two guys making their way onto the ferry, burdened down with surfboards and backpacks.

"Met 'em on the ferry from Penang. Yanks. From Cal-ee-forn-i-ay." Silvan drops his tone. "Oh, and they call me John. As in 'Long John Silvan'."

"John?" He shoots a look at Katrin, who has raised one eyebrow. How dodgy is this guy?

"Yeah," he puts together a big cheesy grin. "You better start calling me John too. Otherwise you'll confuse them."

"No worries," says Jon. He doesn't trust Silvan but he doesn't want to get him offside either. He knows he's dodgy, but he isn't exactly sure what sort of dodgy.

They'd met Silvan on the overnight train from Kuala Lumpur, to Penang. He'd befriended them and shown them to a decent backpackers hostel when they arrived. He was very free with his story, which sounded pretty unlikely. Apparently he was an Australian who'd been away from Australia for twenty years. He might look like a kind of vanilla Charles Manson, but he was a family man, with two kids, happily married to a Swiss woman, with whom he lived in the Swiss Alps. But then he also travelled six months of the year (without them, apparently) and had been everywhere and done everything. It was his umpteenth trip to Sumatra. "It is the most classic of all the tropics," he'd said. "The biggest flower, orang-utans, volcanos, tigers, monstrous surf. Everything is extreme here. They have natural disasters all the time and you never ever hear about them. Dreadful road accidents. Hundreds die in floods and mudslides every year. There's thousands get quietly killed in that little civil war…" He'd woven a good yarn and he'd got Jon and Ethan pretty excited about the trip.

The two younger guys wander over, putting their surfboards down carefully on the deck. "Hey, John, buddy. Who are your friends?" says one in a smooth-sounding American accent. He sounds like someone on TV, thinks Jon.

Silvan makes the introductions and the Americans shake hands with everyone. It seems to Jon that Katrin is the central interest, so he's not terribly friendly to the newcomers. These are not his type of traveller; surfing nuts on the trip to end all trips, to surf the great waves at Nias. And he thinks they're jerks getting about this conservative country in low-slung board shorts with their Hawaiian shirts open exposing their bare chests.

One of them, Cameron, is pretty chatty. "So, John," he says, "you got this sorted as to where we get offa this boat?"

For some unknown reason, Silvan thinks this is an excuse to lay a big wink on Katrin. "Leave it to me. I got just the place in mind. Was there about three years ago. I'll know it when I see it." He explains that the ferry from Parapat to Samosir Island skims around the coast stopping at all the guest houses.

"Where are you guys staying?" Cameron asks Katrin.

She hesitates a second. "Jon has a place in mind," she says.

Jon doesn't volunteer, so Cameron prompts him. "So, Jon, where y'headin'?"

"Maybe Bagus Bay. Or Tabo," says Jon.

"That where we're goin'?" he asks Silvan.

Silvan shakes his head. "Nope. Been there. Not really my thing."

"Well, maybe we'll catch up while we're here," says Cameron.

Jon's relieved to see them get off. After his stuff-up last night, he wouldn't blame Katrin if she took up with someone else. And what guy wouldn't think she was awesome.

He's kicking himself about what a mess of it he made. These European girls are so much cooler than the one's he's known back home. She'd been so nice about what happened. She must have known how crap he was feeling, but she made sure to reassure him, telling him she still wanted to be his friend.

He knows he should try to explain, but he isn't sure what he can say that won't lower her opinion of him further. While he's trying to sort that one out, he's kind of stunned into silence.

What a relief that she's not going to take up with some broad-shouldered boy bimbo like Cameron. And Silvan! He's dreamin'. You gotta despise old men who chase around after girls young enough to be their granddaughter.

He's pleased that the ferry is dropping them off last. It's given him a chance to get his bearings from the water. Lake Toba – or Danau Toba – as the Indonesians call it – is truly spectacular. Formed by a massive volcano that exploded about a hundred thousand years ago – yes, he read his Lonely Planet – it is the largest lake in south east Asia. It's about a hundred kilometres long and three or four hundred metres deep.

Sometime after the original volcano erupted, there was another volcanic eruption and an island formed in the lake. It too is massive. His guide book says it's as big as the whole island of Singapore. There is a narrow strip of land around its edges, like a shelf, which is at water level. Just a few hundred metres inland, though, a very steep hillside rises up to a plateau, eight hundred metres above the water level. The plateau is massive and takes up most of the island – only, if you read the fine print, it's not a real island, because it is actually joined to the outer walls of the crater, by a narrow strip of land.

Anyway, no one much cares about that. The place is called an island – Pulau (the Indonesian word for island) Samosir.

Now the ferry is taking them around just a tiny little bit of it, a little knobby peninsula called Tuk-Tuk. Even though there's some tourist stuff in other places, this is the main tourist area. It's like a little mushroom-shaped protrusion of flat land that juts out a few hundred metres from the main bulk of the island. Hotels, bars and restaurants are gathered pretty much one after another right around the banks.

The young tout is back again now that Silvan is gone. He'd approached them earlier, trying to get them to stay at his guest house, but Silvan told him to piss off. A bit too rudely, for Jon's liking. Jon almost wants to stay at his place to make up for it, but he's also thinking he likes the sound of the vegetarian place, Tabo. Especially given the pig incident. But these guys are from Linda's next door.

The name doesn't do much for him. Linda's. Sounds boring. But Koko, the one doing all the talking, is saying a room with hot water is only ten thousand and it's right on the water. He feels sorry for Koko. He's just a young bloke and his job is going back and forth on the ferries each day "hunting tourists" as he himself put it. He chatted with him and Koko's very friendly. He tells him that he doesn't get a wage – just room and board. Jon reckons he must get some kind of commission for getting tourists into rooms, but it couldn't be much if the rooms are only two dollars a night. Koko says he gets cash from renting out his motorbike, or doing a tour. But pretty much he doesn't have any money. He's extremely laid back and happy, though, and Jon kind of likes him. This must have been what life was like for his father at seventeen. Then along comes Sharon. Ten years older. Cashed-up. World-wise. It must have been pretty exciting for him.

As the ferry comes in, Koko points out Tabo and Linda's. They're right next door to each other and they can get off the ferry and check out both quite easily. Koko follows them to the edge of Tabo and waits for them, till they're back a few minutes later. Tabo's pretty nice, but a bit fancy and quite expensive, relatively speaking. Well, twenty dollars a night expensive.

Linda's, on the other hand is perfect. They take three rooms. They're next to each other, Jon at one end, Ethan in the middle and Katrin at the other end. They're all set up like terrace houses looking out over the water. It's late afternoon and the sun is casting a beautiful deep blue light over the lake. There's a fisherman out there in a canoe setting his nets. In the distance the walls of the Samosir plateau tower as a backdrop, a lush tropical green. The view is breathtaking.

Each room has a little table and chair out the front. Jon plonks himself down. This is where I was conceived, he thinks. I started my life here. Half my ancestors are from this place. Their bones are buried in this soil.

I've come back and I feel like I could stay here forever.

12

Pulau Samosir

Ethan thinks this is the closest to perfect happiness he's ever been.

He raises the bottle of Bintang to his lips. Beads of moisture run down the side. There's a trace of the ice left on the outside. Just a trace. But the contents are still bitingly cold. He sucks down the cool amber ale.

There's a mellow fuzziness in his head. Warm sun beats down on his bare arms and legs.

Leaning back in the canoe, he trails an arm out the side, and looks out over the lake. Resting his head on the sides of the canoe he watches as the land bobs up and down as the boat shifts on the gentle lake ripples.

Koko is in the water and the canoe rocks violently as he grabs hold of the side and hauls himself in. A gallon of water empties off him and into the boat, but it's drying almost instantly.

Koko is wearing cut-down jeans and no shirt, and his brown skin glistens with water and sun. Ethan watches him as he digs a plastic bag out.

He has a ready-made joint in there. He lifts it to show Ethan. "*Ganjah*, Ethan! You like?"

Ethan isn't surprised. He smelt it last night when he passed the boys' room. "Na, mate. I'll stick to beer." He raises the bottle and takes a great big swig. The sun is making him thirsty. Perhaps he should have asked Koko to get him more beer. He'd given him money and Koko had iced the beer for him in the hotel freezer.

Koko lights the joint and blows a thick cloud of smoke across the canoe. It smells sweet, like Kretek, but more familiar.

It's a good spot to be smoking it, out here on the lake. If the police came, you'd see them a mile off.

Ethan is scared of dope. He knows Indonesia has the death penalty and that you can get it for drugs. He is terrified of the idea of capital punishment.

He also personally doesn't like it much. The first time he had it was when Sharon first got sick. Some mates had said it'd relax him. But nothing happened. Nothing at all. Maybe he hadn't had enough. Maybe he'd smoked it wrong. He wasn't that good at the draw back with regular smokes. That was in grade six, just before he started high school.

The next time he had it was out of a bong. They were down by Merri Creek, near the railway bridge. There were about six of them, all year seven boys. He watched how the others did it and when it was his turn he sucked the smoke in till he thought his lungs would burst. Then he coughed and spluttered as the heat hit his lungs. His friends thought it was hysterical. As he sucked down some Coke, the effect came on. It was close to instantaneous. And it wasn't pleasant.

He felt frightened. He kept thinking of that boy who was murdered by primary school kids in England. That had been by a railroad track. And the more he looked at his friends the more he became worried about why they'd asked him down here.

He did nothing. He couldn't speak.

Soon they were all laughing hysterically but him. He tried to join in.

Then he said he was going for a piss. He ran away. Ran all the way home.

But he'd persisted. He didn't know any boys who didn't like dope. The time after that he'd bought some and smoked it by himself, when Jon was at work and Sharon was asleep. He blew the smoke out his window. The feeling was similar, but different. He worried that Sharon would die and that Jon would leave him. He'd found himself almost paralysed with fear. He'd not touched dope since.

As they get drunker, they play a version of I spy. It's silly and makes no sense. Koko is stoned and Ethan is half pissed. He teaches Koko to say "I spy with my little eye….something beginning with…" then Koko says the letter, but for the Indonesian word. Ethan's Indonesian is very limited, so he can never guess the word. Koko has to tell him. He does clouds, hills, water, boat, sun, paddle, bird and then moves on to body parts. The game drops away and they just start trading names for head, eye, arm.

Ethan says, "*Apa ini?* What's this?' and points to his foot.

"*Kaki!*" says Koko.

Ethan points to his leg. "*Apa ini?*"

"*Kaki!*" says Koko.

"*Kaki?*" Ethan points to his foot. Then moves to his leg. "*Kaki?*"

"*Kaki! Kaki!*" Koko finds this hysterical. "Same word foot and leg." He's laughing his head off. Must be the dope. It's not that funny.

Koko points to his hand, "*Tangan,*" he says.

"*Tangan,*" Ethan repeats.

Koko points to his arm. He starts laughing before he speaks and he can barely get the word out. "*Tangan!*" he says. "*Tangan dan tangan!*" He rolls sideways into the bottom of the boat holding his ribs as he laughs.

This conversation is getting idiotic, Ethan thinks.

The beer is getting to him. He stands unsteadily and adjusts his shorts so he can piss over the side.

When he turns round, Koko has grabbed the beer and is taking a long swig. He's sitting in the bottom of the boat in a puddle of water his back against the seat for support.

"*Apa ini?*" Koko says and he's pointing to his crotch.

Ethan's thinking of those touchy-feely guys on the top of the bus. I'm not sure I like where this is heading, he thinks.

"You tell me," he says. "What's it called in bahasa?"

"*Zakar!*"

"Huh?"

"*Alat laki-laki.*" Koko's cracked up again.

Ethan knows *laki-laki* – it means "male". "What's *alat* mean?" He knows he's heard it before.

Koko understands, but he can't remember. He knocks his knuckle against his head. "Like this" – he points to the paddle.

"Paddle?" It's called a "male paddle"? This is ridiculous.

"No, no! Also the word for this." Koko points to a kind of metal thing, like a shovel, that is lying in the bottom of the boat. "Also this." He makes a motion of hammering a nail, then sawing a plank.

"Tool!" shouts Ethan. Now that is funny.

"And in *Inggris*," says Koko, "I know!" He can barely speak he's laughing so much. "Luflud!" he roars.

"Huh?"

"Luflud?"

Ethan frowns. "I don't think so."

"Lurf rud? Lof rod? Luf rod!"

Ethan gets it. Indonesians don't use the letter "v".

What kind of demented seventies porn star taught poor Koko that.

Sometimes Jon worries that he might get addicted to running. He loves the feeling of his lungs working hard, his body pounding along in a steady fast rhythm. Often he runs in his dreams. In them he's very powerful and highly mobile. He charges up and down mountains effortlessly and at great pace, covering enormous distances and never tiring. The dreams are exhilarating. He's never dreamed of flying, but he thinks it would be similar.

He runs nearly everyday. Actually, he sometimes has to stop himself running more than once a day. But since he's been travelling he's missed a few days. He isn't sure why.

At home he used to love to run at night, especially in the rain. He loves the feeling of rain on his face and if it's cold, he loves the burn it makes in his lungs. He usually listens to music. Something atmospheric, with a beat, but hypnotic. Trance music sometimes. Chilli Peppers. He must ask Katrin what she's got on her MP3 player. If he likes it, maybe they can burn it at one of the internet cafés.

Sometimes, though, it's even better running in the heat of the day, like he is now. Normally he likes to run bare-chested. Although it's hot, he likes the warmth of the sun on his skin, the feeling of it burning away his sweat as soon as it forms.

Right now he's wearing a T-shirt. He also has on shorts and runners and around his waist is a pouch containing the essentials he couldn't stand to loose, his passport and return ticket, his insurance policy, his ATM card and the key to his room. Jon rarely ever lets these items out of his sight because he knows it'll be a nightmare if he loses them.

He's got his day pack too. That's why he's got the T-shirt on – and inside is a pair of microlight long pants and a short-sleeved shirt. It's his change of clothing.

Maybe he'll meet his father today. He wants to make a reasonable impression.

He's a very good runner, so he knows that in about an hour he'll cover quite a bit of ground. He wants to run out towards Tomok, the neighbouring village, and just get a picture in his head of what it is like. He won't stop – not dressed like this – but it won't hurt to know what it's like before he gets there later.

This has got to be the best way to see Lake Toba. As he runs up out of Tuk-Tuk the road winds about, rising gently above the lake. The sun is bright overhead and there's only just some wisps of cloud in the sky. It's quiet. There are a few people about. A woman uses a bunch of straw as a broom to sweep the front of her house. Some children, too young for school, are playing with a puppy. As he leaves Tuk-Tuk the houses change to paddocks and rice fields. A water buffalo lies wallowing in mud, a long grey rope tethering it to a stake hammered into the ground. A farmer stands thigh deep in a wet rice field, planting the rice strand by strand.

Everywhere to his left there is the awesome lake stretching out for kilometres, a flat blue expanse glistening in the sunlight. In the distance the ancient walls of the crater, five hundred metres high, smooth, green and nearly treeless, ring the water. Koko's uncle told him about the time the loggers had come and taken all the trees. It had been jungle, when he was a boy, he'd said.

About fifteen minutes into his run, he's out of Tuk-Tuk and he's turned left onto the main road that winds around the island. A short distance further and he's in some trees, then crossing a bridge. It's cool in here, a relief from the sun that's heating the bitumen to the point where Jon's feeling it through the soles of his shoes.

He pounds on, trying not to break the rhythm, just jogging straight through Tomok, where Koko seemed to think the Subawa family were from. He is glad to be able to check it out without stopping. It's very quiet and in a couple of minutes he's charged out the other side of town and he's running along the coast road again.

Half an hour later, he's floating on his back, listening to his heart rate returning to normal. This is the most amazing water he's ever swum in. It's clear like sea water, but fresh like from a spring. He breaks all the rules to gulp down several delicious cool mouthfuls.

Soon, though, he climbs out and dries off in the sun. Then he dresses and walks back into Tomok.

He's nervous, so he stops the first chance he gets and asks someone. It's all done in his fairly ordinary Indonesian.

"*Selamat Pagi Pak,*" he says to a man who looks about his father's age.

"*Selamat Pagi!*"

"*Di mana rumah Pak Darwin Subawa?* Where is the house of Darwin Subawa?"

Jon doesn't understand the old man's response, but he's waving him off as if he's really annoyed, so Jon moves along. He's looking for someone else to ask, but there's no one else around. He's almost to the edge of the village when a man on a motor scooter pulls up.

"You want Darwin Subawa?" he says, over the top of the rattle of the little two-stroke engine.

"Yes! You know him?"

"My cousin." The man's English is rusty, but he speaks carefully, each word spoken with precision.

"Where is he?"

"Not here."

"Where?"

"Why you want him?"

Jon's thought this out already "I have some money for him. From a friend."

"You give to me?"

"No. Where is he?"

The man hesitates, but only for a second. "Bukit Lawang," he says. "You want rent scooter?"

13

To Ambarita and the Central Highlands

If it looks like a duck and quacks like a duck, then it probably is a duck. Except, of course, if it's an imitation duck like this piece-of-crap pretend mountain bike that Ethan's hired for fifty cents a day. He's only been on it for fifteen minutes, but the problems are pretty obvious. The cranks are way too short. He feels like he's beating an egg, here. He pumps his legs madly, just to get over the smallest of hills, but he can't get any rhythm. He's going to get blisters from his knees knocking together.

The whole thing is built entirely wrong. It's got the nobby wheels and straight handlebar and the right kind of general shape, but the cranks seem too close to the seat, so he's all scrunched up. He's put the seat up to its limit so that his knees aren't up against his chest, but all it's done is made the handlebars too low. He'd tried to adjust them up, but they're already at their maximum height.

Lucky the road around the island is pretty flat. And mostly it's a proper made road, because this mountain bike has no suspension at all. Every bump he goes over seems destined to make him less of a man.

Still, he's having a fairly good morning. He likes being out on the road, moving about under his own steam rather than having to catch buses and bemos and motorcycle taxis everywhere. Jon and Katrin are close by, each riding their own identical duck and they're having similar problems. He's already helped Katrin adjust her seat, but as she's about the same height as him it won't have helped much. Jon looks like he's riding a BMX, the bike is so wrong for him.

That morning Jon had explained where he wanted to go and shown him a map. Ethan's got a pretty good picture of this place now.

Today they're riding out of Tuk-Tuk to a village called Ambarita. It isn't very far, thankfully, just a couple of kilometres.

As they leave Tuk-Tuk they get to the main road and go right, which puts the lake on their right and the massive hillside leading to the highlands on their left. It's fairly flat and easy riding and the road stays close enough to the coast for the views around every corner to be totally awesome. It's still early, so even though the sun is hot, there's a cool crispness in the air, especially in the shadows.

Katrin pushes to catch up with him. "Hey, how about we stop for coffee?"

"Cool," he says. He'll have a red Fanta and maybe some more guacamole. He's getting kind of addicted to it. Lots of fresh mushy avocado, with chopped tomato and chilli. He likes to have chips – the Indonesians always call them fried potatoes, but they're chips – and dip them in the guacamole. This little feast might set him back a dollar.

Ethan loves this place. You can get a hamburger on freshly baked bun. You can get a real pizza. All the shops do chips, but they're fresh, chopped from real potatoes.

There's a big screen TV down at Bagus Bay where they play new release DVDs and they even have a pool table.

But there are almost no tourists. They are the only guests at Linda's. You walk around the streets and see no one. But it's kind of fun. The staff come and sit down at your table. Last night Koko and his mates had brought their guitars and he and Jon and Katrin sat around with Theresa, the lady who runs Linda's – doing all the cooking and waiting tables – and sang songs. These Sumatrans are pretty amazing musicians. Koko had a book of about a hundred songs and you could just pick one out and he'd play it and there were the words. It was like karaoke.

"In here," calls Katrin as she turns off the road towards an open air restaurant that has signs for Nescafé and Happy Pizza nailed to a tree beside its drive. It's hard to say why Katrin's chosen it, but it must be their lucky day because when they pull up Silvan is there with his two Californian friends.

The Americans have ordered a Happy Pizza. They're supposedly made with magic mushrooms, which have a similar effect to LSD. Silvan isn't having one. Even though it's only morning, he's having a beer.

Ethan doesn't feel like beer this morning and he's certainly not interested in the mushroom pizzas. He can't imagine much worse than LSD. He's heard it can flip you out so you see things that aren't there, like you're covered in spiders. He's even heard that people sometimes cut themselves thinking stuff has crawled inside their veins. But those big dumb Yanks are sitting there talking up the experience, like they can't wait for the ride. The good-looking one is Cameron. He really fancies himself. And then there's Dave, who Ethan reckons is as thick as two planks. Cameron's latched on to Dave because he makes him look like the better option, Ethan's thinking.

As the pizzas come out, Ethan's watching them with mild disgust. These are grown men and the way they're carrying on – all excited making panting noises and groaning like they're horny, except for a mixture of pizza and drugs – they think they're being cool, but it's just plain embarrassing. Ethan's only fourteen – half a decade younger than these guys – but no fourteen-year-old he knows would be seen like this.

He orders guacamole, fried eggs and chips and a mango pancake. That's the other thing you have to love about Sumatra. You order whatever you like and they make it. No questions asked. If he wants curry and rice for breakfast, he'll have it. If it's fried eggs and chips, no problems. Pancake with banana, chocolate and – let's see – coconut. Easy.

He's in a really awesome mood. In fact he's surprised himself. He's actually been looking forward to this bike ride. Later they're going to scale that hillside and stay in a real village up on top. He even had a read in the guidebook about it, which is amazing for him. He feels like he's been lazing about here for three days and now he wants to do something. Jon's lightened right up too, which has made life better. So Ethan's been getting Koko to get him beer whenever he likes, and he's been fishing and paddling and swimming and sunbaking.

Jon's also in a good mood. All right, so he hasn't found his father, but he does know where he is and that he's alive. That's a massive move in the right direction. The motor scooter man had eventually taken him back to his house. Jon didn't let on who he was, but maybe he suspected because over an hour or so, he had introduced him to a bunch of people who were apparently distant relatives. He asked about *Ayah* and *Ibu Darwin* – Darwin's parents – his grandparents. But he was told they were "*sudah meninggal,* already dead".

But he'd found out something else, that's really got his mind buzzing. He has a sister. She's around five, his cousin thinks. Darwin has married a Muslim woman and converted. He now lives in her village near Bohorok and works somewhere at Bukit Lawang. Jon's turning over images in his mind of all the people he met: could one of them be his father? Surely he'd have recognised him?

He isn't sure. But now he knows he's almost certain to meet him within a few days. He's incredibly excited, but also nervous.

But the closer he gets to finding his old man, the harder it gets to talk to Ethan about it. It must be pretty strange for him – Jon about to find his father, but Ethan still being on his own – except for Jon, of course. But you'd never know it bothered him. When Jon updates him on what he's learned, he just says something like "Cool" or "No worries" or 'Awesome" – one-word answers that are not exactly negative, but at the same time don't really tell Jon a lot about what Ethan is thinking.

There's no point in worrying, though – it's all going to happen pretty soon.

He and Katrin have hatched a good plan. As she is on her way out of Sumatra, they'll stay at Lake Toba for two more days and do some things she wants to do. Then the three of them will go back to Bukit Lawang. She'll meet her friends and do her trek. He'll meet his father. By the time she's back, he'll have some idea about what he wants to do then. If things are going well, he and Ethan might stay there a while. Secretly he's really hoping that happens. He'd love to have Ethan in a Muslim village for a while away from the temptations of booze.

But Jon's no fool. He knows things may not go well with his father.

He's prepared himself for that, as much as he can. If it doesn't work, they can leave with Katrin and maybe go with her to Thailand. Actually, he hasn't quite got so far as discussing that part with her.

The pizza still hasn't kicked in when they leave the Californian boys. Maybe it's a dud, thinks Ethan.

Riding on a little they reach a big cluster of shops. There are dozens of them one after another down both sides of the street. There are way too many to count. They're all open for business, though there's hardly anybody working in them. It doesn't look like a tourist has been here in years.

The shops are weird, because they're all almost identical to each other. They're all open-fronted places and each is full of thousands and thousands of wood carvings. Most are intricately carved with great skill. There's masks and bowls and spears and human figures – female and male – in various states of nudity. There's all sorts of animal ornaments, everything from small frogs to tigers, elephants and giant monitor lizards a metre long.

He takes this in quickly. It's quite overwhelming. He'd like to stop, but instead they slow down and glide past, conscious that there are no customers here and it's unlikely there will be any anytime soon. If you stopped to look, they'd get so excited you'll feel pretty much obliged to buy something.

It's kind of sad, really. All these cleverly made objects. Presumably in villages somewhere there are carvers making more clever things and wondering why no one wants them. You get the feeling that this place was once much busier, with hundred of tourists. There's something almost eerie about it now.

Not half so eerie as what they see next. Minutes later they're in Ambarita and Jon seems to have got them to the place they're looking for. The execution chairs. He's even found them a guide who speaks English. For ten thousand rupiah he's showing them around and filling in the gaps.

The chairs are carved white stone. They're pretty rough and ready village-style chairs, and they are in a circle maybe five metres across. They look ancient, but they're more like hundreds of years old – so their guide tells them. And of course, they're not in use any more.

It's kind of a village courtroom and execution chamber rolled into one. The accusers and judges sit with the condemned person and watch him or her die. Maybe they're tied to the chair or held down, of maybe some were very brave and just sat there. But the executioner would come over and kill them with a knife. Ethan sits in the chair. He's trying to soak up the atmosphere and wondering if he'll be able to sense anything – y'know, like the Sixth Sense – but he doesn't feel much.

After that they're taken through a long house. It's pretty amazing. A big wooden house with a freaky sloping roof that looks like the horns of a giant buffalo. Inside it's dark and smoky from the fire that they keep going. The guide tells them that lots of families live in here together. Ethan wonders about sex. How do they do it with everyone around all the time?

Later than night he's thinking about sex again. Jon's arse is sticking into him. He's just tried to shove him over, but Jon's elbowed him. Now Jon's sncring and Ethan knows he'll never get to sleep.

So he's thinking about sex, and why Jon and Katrin don't seem to be having it any more.

He and Jon are in this room at Jenny's Guest House, at the village of Dolok, up on top of the plateau. It isn't a village like you'd think of a village. There's no shop, although Jenny sells soft drink, beer and simple meals. There's just three wooden houses.

The climb up here was devastating. Three hours straight up. His calf muscles started burning in the first twenty minutes. Even though they got in about four this afternoon, his legs were still wobbling when he stumbled into bed tonight.

But what a view. From eight hundred metres high, the lake is a knockout. Tuk-Tuk looks likes a map, down below.

Jenny's guest house has just three rooms and they cost thirty cents a night each. There's no electricity, no running water, and no toilet. On the edge of the village someone has erected a platform and enclosed it in planks, for privacy. There's a sign "Tourist Toilet" nailed onto it, which should be warning enough. There's a hole in the floor and the waste splats about a metre below on the grass. Basically it'd be fully disgusting, if there were more tourists. But as there aren't, it doesn't bother him. He doesn't know what the locals do for a toilet. There doesn't seem to be one.

But the beds are comfortable. It's cold up here so there are lots of blankets. And it's very dark so you don't get to look too closely at anything, which is probably just as well in a place with no running water or power.

Ethan really loves it here, but he can't say why. The beer and soft drink is warm. That'd been a shock after that climb. Warm beer! Not nice at all – he'd passed on it and had warm Coke instead. But it's all pretty impressive when you think everything here has probably been carried up that monstrous hillside in a crate by someone – almost certainly a woman – as they seem to do so much of the grunt work here. About halfway up they'd been overtaken by an old woman with red teeth and a basket of fresh lake fish on her head. She'd stopped when Katrin offered her an Oreo cookie. Jon had been able to talk Indonesian with her. She went to market and back three times a week, up and down that hillside in tough sun-browned bare feet. She went on ahead, but waited up top and walked with Jon a little way trying to sell him a fish. They'd come across a stream with a thick bamboo pole slung across it. The old lady went over tightrope-style, her bare feet perfect for the task. Then seeing their hesitation, she came back to lead Katrin across, taking her hand and steadying her, fish still on her head. Ethan and Jon had waved her off – no old lady was going to walk them across like they were kindergarten kids. But they paid for their arrogance with wet runners as first Jon, then Ethan slipped ungracefully into the water. It wasn't deep. The water was cool and refreshing and squelching shoes weren't worth worrying too much about. It'd been pretty funny too – they had all laughed. Then they gave the old lady a crumpled one-thousand-rupiah note – about twenty cents – for helping Katrin. She smiled her red grin and waved goodbye, as if she thought it was her lucky day.

Maybe it was. Everything was very cheap up here. Dinner cost them two thousand rupiah each. The food up here at Jenny's is "family food" – just what the family eats. Jenny had met them in the yard and said, "You want chicken?" There'd been an axe in one hand and a chicken dangling by its feet in the other.

What do you say in that situation? Ethan didn't want to be responsible for the slaughter of the chicken. But how do you explain that? Jon had paid extra to get something vegetarian – he never seems to eat meat any more. But Ethan ended up eating the chicken. Poor thing was delicious.

After dinner they'd sat around a little bored, but too tired to do anything much to liven things up. There's no TV. No radio or CD player. There's hardly even any people. Just Jenny and her husband – and all their evenings in candlelight. Guests from overseas make their lives different from most people up here, but they keep to themselves. Jenny's husband played his guitar for a while in the next room. That was pleasant, but it's weird listening to live music when you can't see it. And when he stopped it was absolutely silent.

So they'd gone to bed early. Like at about eight p.m.

And now all he can hear is Jon's snoring and the occasional sounds of rats under the floorboards. At least he hopes they're underneath.

Jon mutters something and tries to pull the blankets off onto himself. Ethan holds on tight to stop him until he gives up, muttering in a pissed-off hard-done-by kind of fashion. Jon's in Ethan's bed because he's not with Katrin and because there's some crazy Austrian traveller staying up here who's been in the third room for six weeks.

They'd heard about Tomas down at Linda's. He was something of a myth about the place. Apparently a rumour was going around that some Western guy had fallen in love with a local woman up there and showed no signs of leaving.

From what Ethan could see, it was true. Tomas seemed very settled at Jenny's. In the evening he got out his German–Indonesian dictionary and started studying. He spoke no English, so Jon chatted with him in halting Indonesian and Katrin was able to speak German with him.

His girlfriend seemed to be an open secret, but a rather controversial one. That afternoon Jenny has been looking stressed and had asked where Tomas was and if we'd seen him with her sister. They gathered she meant the other woman who lived next door, as she seemed to be the only other adult female about the village. Ethan had said 'No' – but later Katrin said she saw them walking out into the forest, her first, him following a minute behind. She said it was pretty clear what was happening.

Ethan wishes he were a little more physically comfortable here. If that were the case, he'd like to stay up here at Jenny's for a while. Like Tomas. He could learn Indo properly and meet a girl. This place makes it hard to imagine going back home and back to school. Just in an afternoon he feels like he's left the modern world behind. And with it he's shed his anxieties like a skin. He's curious how living like this would change him – and how quickly – if he let it.

He'll never know, though. Tomorrow it's back down the hillside to the real world.

14

Linda's Guest House, Tuk-Tuk

It's Koko with a bottle of Bintang and the keys to his motorcycle. He holds both up for Ethan to see and raises his eyebrows in a question. Ethan sneaks a look at Jon. He hasn't noticed.

Ethan gives Koko a smile and the thumbs up. Then he points to his wrist – where a watch would be if he wore one – and holds up five fingers to indicate five minutes. Koko gives him the thumbs up back and goes out front to wait.

They're sitting up at Linda's restaurant on the balcony overlooking the lake.

Cameron and Dave are there with Katrin and Jon. Jon's just bought the guys lunch.

Poor bastards, Ethan's thinking. Can't believe that Silvan prick ripped them off.

They'd turned up a couple of hours ago looking for help. They were still sick as dogs, from the mushrooms. A few hours before that they'd woken up in a stinking little hut out the back of the Happy Pizza restaurant. They had little or no memory of the twenty-four hours before that.

"Just lights and the walls pulsating and chucking up for what seems like hours," said Cameron.

Ethan couldn't help but feel a little satisfaction at having been smart enough to avoid those pizzas.

Anyway, it got worse. When they started thinking straight, they wondered where their wallets were. When they couldn't find those, they had to walk back to their hotel as they couldn't afford a motorcycle taxi. When they got there Silvan had already cleared out. He'd left them their surfboards and backpacks, but he'd taken their passports, tickets,

113

money, traveller's cheques, credit cards and cameras. Then he'd put the copies of their insurance policies on Cameron's bed, weighted down with their room key. He'd kindly circled in pen the emergency number they should call. Smart bastard.

"Why our passports?" moans Cameron. "He can't use them, surely."

Katrin had answered, "He'll get them altered. New photograph. Different age, obviously. Maybe a slight name change. What's your surname?"

"Davies," says Cameron.

"Flood," says Dave.

"So they become Davieson and Floody. Or something like that. A lot of these border crossings have only the most basic of passport checks. There's nothing electronic. Just a glance and a stamp. And every guest house wants to see a passport, but they just write down the country and the name and number. He's probably got half a dozen of them he uses as he moves about."

"That story about his Swiss wife..." says Jon.

"Probably just so you wouldn't wonder why an Australian was using a Swiss passport," says Katrin.

"Well, that's our trip completely stuffed..." Cameron mutters.

Katrin slaps him on the shoulder. "Don't worry. Insurance will cover it. Later we'll get the police and make a report."

"Yeah, but we've got nothing. Not even a bus fare to the US consulate to apply for a replacement passport."

"Don't worry,' says Jon. "I'm going to give you fifty bucks. That'll be enough – things are so cheap here. You can go to Medan, or even Jakarta if you have to. Once you're in a city you can get your folks to wire money to a bank, or something."

"Hey, man, thanks. That's real generous..."

"Well, you'll get it back to me. Plus I should have said something to you. There was something not right about him."

That had surprised Ethan. He'd liked Silvan. He'd thought he was funny and cool. He'd happily slept in the bunk between Silvan and Jon back in Penang when they'd taken dorm beds. He'd barely given it a second thought when Jon had asked him to give him the pouch containing his passport and ticket. Jon had slept with both of their pouches around his waist, under his clothes.

Now he's finding the idea of the old man lying next to him as he slept really creepy. Did his fingers slip around Ethan's waist checking for stuff during the night? He doesn't know and that's not a great feeling at all. For some reason he can't get out of his head the image of Silvan lying there awake while he slept.

Thank God for Jon, he's thinking. He's got to give Jon credit. He wouldn't have lasted one night without him. He was like a sitting duck for the likes of Silvan. And their trip would have stopped right there. He'd looked over at Jon with a little more respect.

But he's got plans for today and he'd better get going. Right now Jon's distracted and Ethan seizes the moment, saying, "Hey, catch you guys later. Koko and I are going down to Bagus Bay to play pool."

Moments later he's on the back of Koko's scooter wearing a construction helmet without a strap, and they're roaring off down the road.

This is not just about drinking. Koko's going to take him right around the island on his scooter. They're going to go visit some of Koko's mates, so it'll be kind of cultural. And go to some parts he hasn't seen yet. A bit more geography and history. Also they'll stop for some beers at some nice spots. It's Ethan's job to pay for the food and drinks for the both of them. And he's also going to give Koko about two dollars for the afternoon.

He takes a swig on the beer as they ride along. Koko's riding pretty slowly, so Ethan can drink and check out the scenery as they go. They take the road out of town that they rode bicycles on and whip past the Happy Pizza restaurant where Silvan had woven his little rip-off, and on through Ambarita in a matter of minutes. As the road winds on, hugging the coast, Ethan is surprised at how many empty guest houses and restaurants there are. You think it all stops at Tuk-Tuk, but it doesn't. There's lots of empty-looking places built along the edges of the lake.

"You want some of this?" he says into Koko's ear.

"Nah. Later," Koko says, then revs the little bike hard and leans into a corner.

Ethan doesn't want to, but he's forced to put a steadying hand down on Koko's hip. Koko laughs and Ethan isn't exactly sure why. As the bike straightens up, Ethan reaches back and grasps for a bar to hold on to. There isn't one, so he returns his hand to Koko's waist.

Soon the beer is gone and Ethan needs a piss. So he calls out to Koko to stop.

"OK, OK. Happy Pizza Two! Just here!"

Koko swerves down a dirt track and seconds later they're pulling up outside a shed with an attached wooden platform. On the platform are three old laminex tables and a collection of dusty plastic stools. Koko pulls the scooter up onto its stand and they sit their helmets on the handle bars. Koko's has a strap, he notices. That might actually make it useful for something other than falling coconuts.

Ethan makes a quick dash to the kamar kecil – another series of planks with a hole in the middle, this time surrounded by hessian cloth nailed to a frame on two sides. Oh well, it's functional. And it's got a great view of the lake.

Back at the table he grabs a stool across a table from Koko. He barely has time to light a smoke before a crotchety old man with skinny bowed legs and a massive forward bend in his back comes out. Ethan's seen a lot of old people like that in Sumatra. And when you see the hard lives they lead, hours of bending over planting rice, you can see why.

"Bintang, *Pak*," says Koko.

"*Dua?*" the old man asks hopefully.

Ethan wonders how long since he's sold a beer.

Koko looks at Ethan, because he's buying.

"*Ya, dua,*" says Ethan. "*Dua botel dingin.* Two cold bottles.'

The old man rattles off something too quick for Ethan to catch, or maybe he was speaking the local Batak language.

Koko translates, into the half-Bahasa half-English they've fallen into. "No cold. No *listrik*. Ethan want *es*?"

Beer and ice. Why not?

First the two bottles come out and two dusty glasses. Then the ice. It's a big slab, about the size of a two house bricks. It looks seriously heavy and Ethan can't believe that the poor old man can carry it and walk bent at that angle, without falling flat on his face. But he's got it sorted. He's wrapped a rag around the ice to protect his hands and he's even managed to hold a hatchet while he's carting it out here.

"*Es* safe?" Ethan asks Koko.

The Lonely Planet always warns you about the ice. Apparently some people have been known to make it in their own fridges from unhygienic water straight out of the tap. It can make the humble fruit shake a toxic nightmare.

"Ya, ya. Safe. He collect this morning from *pabrik es*, ice factory."

Of course, it is, thinks Ethan. The poor bastard hasn't got any electricity. How's he gunna make ice…

The slab of ice is put in the centre of the table and the old man starts hacking at it with the hatchet, right there in front of them. Slivers and chunks come off, which the old man scoops up off the table surface with his wrinkly fingers and drops in the glasses, with a series of clinking noises.

When the glasses are three-quarters full, Ethan says, "*Terima Kasih, Pak*. Thank you, sir," and the old man leaves them to pour their own drinks over the top.

It's a delicate operation. Ice seems to increase the fizz. But a few moments later, sipping on his beer slurpee, he wonders why no one puts ice in beer back home. It's beautiful and cold and, as long as you drink it quickly, before too much ice melts, you don't have to worry about the beer getting all watery.

Soon it's gone and Ethan's starting to feel nicely tanked. He has another visit to the kamar kecil and then they're back on the bike.

Now he's more relaxed from the beer and he's enjoying leaning into these bends. Really enjoying it. His mind starts to drift. They're leaving soon. Katrin's heading off to meet her friends at Bukit Lawang and that's where Jon's father is supposed to be. Jon's all keen to go too, even though they've already been there once. Ethan can understand why, he'd just rather stay here, that's all.

And then Ethan sees something that snaps him back to the here and now.

Silvan. It had to be. That white hair.

He's a fair distance off and there's a fair amount of trees between them on the road and the man walking along the path. But Ethan knows it's him.

Looking around quickly, Ethan sees what's going on. Silvan is carrying a plastic bag. There was a shop back a little that sold cigarettes, beer and other stuff. Just down this path he can just see a tiny, rather run-down-looking guest house right on the banks of the lake. It's right back off the road and almost out of sight.

They'd just assumed Silvan had made a break for it the way he'd come in, via the tourist ferry and a bus from Parapat. But what they'd forgotten is that he knows this place and knows it well. He'd just taken a room (probably in another name) somewhere no one would be looking for him. And when the fuss has died down and there's no chance the police will try to intercept buses heading out of here, he'll move on in safety.

Ethan's really pumped now. The beer has gone to his head, and he's up for the challenge. "Hey, Koko. Pull over, man," he says once they are past Silvan. This is cool. There's no way the old prick would have seen them. He tries to explain to Koko what's going on.

"Hey, no *polisi*. We go back to Tuk-Tuk. Then you talk to *polisi sendiri*, by yourself.'

"He might get away."

"Nah. He stay here. He stay here until *polisi* not looking, then go."

But Ethan's decided. He won't wait and he doesn't want the cops. This'll be fun, he's thinking. "You wait for me here," he says.

"Ethan, it's too far. It'll take half an hour to walk down there and back."

"Then drive me down. Drop me off nearby. I'll give you twenty thousand for two more beers."

Koko looks doubtful, but he's weakening.

"Come on, Koko. All ya need to do is buy the beer and ride up the drive again. I'll meet you at the top."

A few minutes later he's slipping off the back of the scooter as it idles noisily halfway down the long drive way. There's no way they could be seen from the guest house through the trees which cluster densely around them.

Ethan's heart is pounding. He's not sure what he's going to do, but it definitely involves ripping Silvan off like he ripped off the Californians. He hasn't decided yet how much he's going to take – whether he's just going to get back the guys' stuff, or whether he's going to teach Silvan a big lesson and leave him stranded with nothing.

As Koko rides off down the hill, Ethan starts to jog parallel to the driveway, but in the trees where he won't be seen. It's hard work. He's thirsty and it's hot and the beer's made him feel really sluggish.

Ethan hears the engine of the scooter stop. He must be down the bottom near the guest house now and Ethan stops for a second. He's going to wait for him to come back up with the beer.

It doesn't take long. He flags Koko down and takes one of the beers off him. "Go wait for me," he says. "I'll be ten minutes, tops."

"*Hati-hati!*" says Koko as he rides off.

Ethan cracks the top off the bottle on the side of a tree and takes a long swig. Then another. He's so thirsty. And the beer's making him feel really good.

He downs most of it as he walks down the last of the hill. Now he's just inside the tree line. He saves the last few gulps of beer for afterwards, leaving the bottle propped up under a tree.

There's no one about. There's a wooden building with a sandy-floored annex built of corrugated iron and wood. It's a bit like Happy Pizza Two, with its random stools and tables, but there's also a hammock.

And there's two large brown feet poking out one end.

Ethan walks closer.

It might be Silvan, but it could also be anyone.

A few yards away there are three or four roughly built bamboo huts, with thatched roofs and rickety-looking verandas facing the lake.

Silvan must be staying in one of those.

He jogs quietly over to the first and sneaks a look in the window. It's dark, but it looks unoccupied.

Then he spots some clothes on a makeshift line hanging off the second hut. There's Silvan's T-shirt. The Red Bull one from Thailand. And there's his surfboard.

Ethan's at the hut in seconds. There's a cut-off stump just close enough for him to stand on and peer in the window. The room is full of stuff – Silvan's really settled in. Ethan sees a book on the bed, a packet of smokes and an ashtray. His pack lays open.

Where would Silvan keep important stuff?

On him. Like Jon does. He's probably got it round his waist right now. But if he's got half a dozen passports and cameras and stuff, he must have another place.

The room is locked, but the window is just a shutter type thing with no glass. And it's been propped wide open to let in a breeze. Silvan probably knows he's the only guest and he's not worried about stuff getting nicked.

Ethan scrambles in the window. It takes only seconds to look under the pillow and the bed.

Where now?

His head is feeling increasingly fuzzy. This is a really dumb idea, he's thinking. Why didn't I just get the cops? They'd be here by now.

But he'd had this image of walking back into Linda's guest house with the Californian boys' stuff. He'd been pretty laid back, but he could see everyone was impressed.

You don't get this kind of opportunity very often. Wasn't going to waste it, now was he?

He rummages through Silvan's pack, but it's just clothes. There's a day pack and inside he finds the two cameras – well at least he finds two very expensive-looking cameras. They could be Silvan's for all he knows, but he's sure they're not and he picks up the pack and slings it over his shoulder.

Silvan's ancient leather bath bag hangs off a doorknob and Ethan looks inside quickly. It's just normal stuff – a comb, shampoo, toothpaste and brush. There's a couple of old-looking condoms, their foil encased in bits of soap and strands of white hair – it isn't a pretty picture – he'd hate to be putting his faith in those! Oh, and there's a straight razor…

That'd be right… Why isn't he surprised?

Still, he doesn't like the look of it much. Who uses a straight razor these days? He drops it back in the bag like a dirty hanky.

Time to leave…

But just before he does he runs a hand down between the mattress of Silvan's bed and the wall. It's the only place left to hide anything.

And he's right. There's a pouch there, jammed right in. It's a decent size – the ridiculously large sort favoured by Americans – the sort they call "fanny packs" without even the hint of a smile. Just right for storing a Lonely Planet or two, which of course old Silvan might need with all his travelling.

Ethan's fingers fumble as he unzips it as quickly as he can.

Bingo.

He doesn't stop to go through everything. Clearly it's what he's looking for. Even Silvan shouldn't have an excuse to have a South African passport, which is the one on the top. And there's several others there too, perhaps five or six, at a glance, plus money, some credit cards and other documents. Ethan re-zips it and shoves it in the day pack with the cameras.

Just then he hears the "crunch, crunch" of feet on the ground outside. The noise changes as they step up onto the veranda. There's a key in the lock. As the door swings open, Ethan's already going head-first out the window.

He jars his shoulder hitting the ground. He scrambles to his feet just as there's a flurry of frantic noises. There's a startled "Hey!" and Silvan appears, charging down the stairs after him. Ethan gets one look at the murderous look in those eyes and he's off, as fast as he can run.

God, he wishes he hadn't had that last beer.

"I'm gunna cut your throat, you little…"

He wishes he'd snatched the blade when he could.

Silvan lunges at him and he feels his hand grasping at his back. He's grabbed a fistful of T-Shirt and Ethan's money belt. He holds on and yanks Ethan backwards.

Sensing what's going to happen, Ethan dives forward, his shirt tearing, the money belt stretching and finally breaking.

Ethan runs. Even half pissed, and sluggish, he's a little faster than Silvan. But he's got stamina, the old man. He doesn't give up.

Ethan's belting up the driveway, like there's no tomorrow. It's long and steep and he's now really feeling the effects of the beer.

A couple of hundred metres up and he's slowed from an all-out sprint to a jog and his lungs are working triple time. He can hear himself. He sounds like he's having an asthma attack.

Actually, he might be having one. This doesn't feel good. He can't get his breath, but he's sure if Silvan gets him he'll kill him. Probably really kill him. Cut his head half off in one slash and sink his body in the lake.

Well, how else would Silvan stop him getting the cops after this? What's he got to lose? He'd do years in a stinking Indonesian prison, just for thieving. The likes of Silvan would surely kill to avoid that.

He hears himself panting. It's a dreadful wheezing sound. He knows he's nearly finished.

Where is Koko? Ethan's getting into a blind panic now.

And Jon'll never know what happened to me… I'll just disappear…

He pushes himself for one last big effort. Rounding the bend he's praying he'll see Koko and the scooter and they can roar away together.

It's there. But it's up on its stand. It's not running and Koko is nowhere to be seen.

Ethan swings to take a look behind. Silvan's fallen back a little. He's about fifty metres back, but still coming.

Ethan stumbles over his own feet and sprawls across the ground coming to rest in front of the scooter. He's got no choice now. He reaches up and the key is there.

Koko will have to hide out till he comes back, because Ethan can't wait.

It happens so quickly. He's on the scooter. It starts with the turn of the key. He rocks it off its stand, puts it into gear and lets out the clutch. Off it goes. Faster than he expected.

He's burned out of the driveway in seconds and out onto the road. He flicks up a gear and roars down the straight, maybe half a kilometre, relief draining through him with the vibration of the two-stroke engine as it takes him further from Silvan with every moment. He leans low and sideways to take the bend.

Oh no! There's no time to stop. He tries to swerve. It's another motor scooter with man, woman and how many kids? They're just going about their business. Ethan's crossed to the wrong side of the road.

They're wobbling trying to avoid him and he's conscious of images and sounds. Like snapshots.

People hitting the bitumen.

The slap of skin.

Someone else's cracking bone.

Children's little bodies flying through the air.

A mother's terrified scream.

Then it's Ethan's body on the line. He hits with a thump that knocks the wind out of him. And then he and the scooter are rolling, over and over.

17

To hospital

There are two reasons he knows his ankle is broken. One, the morphine has worn off and the pain is extraordinary. He simply can't think about anything else while it's going on. Two, the angle it was at when he and the bike finally stopped tumbling over each other. It didn't leave much to the imagination.

Right now he's on a stretcher that Jon has borrowed from the medical centre. Koko has the front and Jon has the back and they're carrying him over a plank and onto the ferry. He's sobered up now, but to go with how busted-up he is, he's got a god-awful hangover. His mouth is dry. His head is pounding. He's wanted to take a shit about four times, but the toilet at the medical centre was a squat toilet and he can't work out how he'd use it with a broken ankle.

The doctor has put a splint on his foot and taped his ribs and sewn up torn skin on his hands and arms, where he'd slammed into the bitumen. Thirty stitches, the doctor had said. God, he hoped everything was sterile. He hadn't looked at the equipment, but Jon was there. Surely he'd checked?

Jon's so angry with Ethan he feels like tipping the stretcher over the side. He can barely speak to him. He wants to shake him for being so bloody stupid.

It's a disaster. Ethan's going to need an X-ray and the foot set and it's all going to cost money. They have insurance, but the insurance won't pay because firstly Ethan is unlicensed and secondly he was drunk. How much can it possibly cost, thinks Jon?

Also, there's the bike, which is probably a write-off. Basically he now needs to buy Koko a new one. There's no way out of that. He wonders what it will cost: a couple of thousand, minimum, he would imagine.

And there's that poor family. None seriously injured – a miracle. How can Ethan live with himself? A drunk driver that put a five-year-old, a three-year-old and their poor parents in hospital. The five-year-old has a broken arm; Jon's been listening to his anguished cries half the night.

Thank God the parents are OK, because there's no social welfare in this country. At least they'll be able to return to work to support themselves and the kids. But Jon'll be paying thousands for their busted bike and the medical bills.

Honestly, he can barely even look at his brother.

Silvan had even got away. By the time they told the cops, he was long gone.

And Ethan has now completely fucked up any hope he had with Katrin. They'd been sitting together out the front of their rooms, when Koko had come to tell him of the accident. He'd been getting up the nerve to try again with her – or at least to try to talk to her.

Now, instead of maybe getting together, she'd spent half the night with him at the medical centre. Once it was clear Ethan wasn't seriously hurt, she'd gone back to her room to sleep and pack.

This morning she'd come by the medical centre to see what was happening.

"Not much," Jon had said.

He was pretty grumpy and pissed off, but Katrin had tried to look past it. She'd even offered to go with them to the doctor and miss her friends. He'd said no. That was crazy. It is just a busted ankle. No drama.

Being a medical student, she'd suggested he might need her.

He'd been polite, but he said he couldn't see how. Either it was a simple break and the Indonesian doctor could fix it, or it wasn't and they'd have to fly home to Australia. He'd shrugged. "He's my stupid jerk of a brother. Don't let him wreck your trip too."

In the face of that, she'd gone off to meet her friends at Bukit Lawang. Then off to Malaysia, Thailand or wherever – it didn't matter. It no longer included him. They'd be stuck here for weeks anyway, getting Ethan's new passport organised.

He's just like his mother, is Ethan. Selfish. Jon's gut is hurting he's so angry.

"Drink some water, Ethan," he says, handing him the bottle.

"Thanks," mutters Ethan. "Can ya open it?" There's a layer of sweat over his skin and a tight, pinched look on his face.

Jon knows he's in pain. He's seen that look on his mother's face too.

Jon twists off the lid and Ethan is able to use his good hand to tip the water into his mouth. Dribbles come out both sides, but Jon doesn't mop them up. "You need anything else?" he says.

Ethan's thinking, the toilet would be nice, but he's not quite so desperate as to ask for Jon's help. So he shakes his head. "Where's Katrin?"

"Got the earlier ferry so she didn't miss her bus."

"Oh."

"I'm going for a piss. Koko's right here if you need any-thing."

Right now he wished he was a smoker. It'd give him an excuse to go and stand up front by himself, away from Ethan. So he goes and uses the toilet. Then he wanders down to the end of the boat and makes small talk with some Indonesians.

When he gets back, Ethan's got his eyes shut. Jon doesn't know if he's asleep or just pretending, but he's grateful he doesn't have to talk to him.

Jon knows fifty dollars is too much, but he's paid a man to drive him, Ethan and Koko to the hospital in Medan. It seemed the best place to be once the doctor in Parapat said Ethan's ankle was badly broken. And a private car seemed the best way to get there fast. He sat up front with the driver. Ethan sat across the back seat with his broken ankle on a pillow on Koko's lap. He moaned all the way.

Jon's feeling more sorry for him now, but he's also more worried about what all this will cost.

Now they're at the hospital. They've been several X-rays and Ethan's been admitted to a ward. Right now Ethan's asleep. They gave him some more morphine and he's right out of it. A young doctor who speaks very good English has just come by and he's explaining to Jon that the ankle will need to be pinned.

Jon's hating the sound of this. Serious orthopaedic surgery in a hospital in Medan. "So if it was you and you could have the operation here or in Australia – where would you have it?"

The doctor shrugs as if he doesn't know, but his voice indicates this is a pretty silly question. "Of course Australia. Or maybe Singapore or KL. You have insurance?"

Jon nods. Even though it isn't going to cover this, he doesn't want this doctor thinking he's so dumb as to go travelling without it.

"He is young. If it is done badly he might have many problems. I think you should go home."

"I think so too," says Jon. When he weighs it up, it's the only solution. If they stay here they'll have big medical bills for an operation that might leave Ethan disabled. If they go home, they'll have several thousand to spend on airfares, if they can't change the date on their ticket. But Medicare will cover specialist treatment on the ankle. Hopefully they can change the date of their flight. The Australian consulate will have to step in to deal with the passport issue.

"Oh," says Ethan when he tells him how it is.

Jon's sitting on a plastic chair in the far corner of the room. "That's all you've got to say?" he mutters.

"Oh fuck, man."

"Fuck's right."

For a second Ethan is silent. "I'm sorry," he says.

Jon looks at him. He can't ever recall Ethan ever saying sorry for anything before. But he's too mad to let it go that easily.

"I am! Really."

"Sorry about what?" Jon doesn't want to be conned by one of those "I'm sorry it's worked out like this" non-apologies. He wants Ethan to be really sorry for causing this whole mess.

"Everything. I've totally stuffed everything."

Jon isn't going to argue.

"Those people. That boy's arm. The two bikes… God. And you're not going to see your dad after all."

Jon hadn't thought of that, but suddenly it dawns on him. This is it. The last he's going to see of Indonesia is this hospital. Just a taxi to the airport, a flight to KL and home.

"And Katrin. What about her?"

Jon answers with a wry smile: "There's nothing there, don't worry."

"Yeah, sure. I know you slept together in Berstagi. She's really hot. I know you like her a lot."

Jon looks sheepish. "Yeah, well, I really stuffed it up."

"How?"

"Forget it. We've got to get us sorted out. Your drinking. Where we're gunna live."

"We will. But what about Katrin?"

"No, Ethan. This is fucking serious!"

"I know it is…"

Jon gives in a little. He's no good with these tense discussions. "It's pretty bloody humiliating, I can tell you."

"As bad as your big brother having to help you have a shit?"

Jon smiles. "Yeah, easily."

"You gotta tell me now."

"Well, we kind of started…" Jon stops. He's gone bright red.

Ethan prompts him: "Doing it?"

"Nah, not quite. But it was going that way. And…"

"Come on!"

"I can't!"

"You couldn't…"

He shakes his head, a little flustered now. "No. Not like that. Actually it was weird. As I leaned over her and started to kiss her I kind of flashed back. To when Mum was in hospital. The day before she died…"

Give your Mum a kiss…

Ethan is silent, waiting for him to go on. Eventually he does.

"I don't know what it was. She's the first girl I've been with since. Just feeling her skin against mine… I had this flashback to leaning over Mum to give her a kiss. Y'know?"

"Shit, Jon, that's pretty awful."

"Yeah."

Ethan takes a moment to mull this over. "And Katrin's all freaked out 'cause she thinks making out with her reminds you of your dead mother. Well, you can kind of understand that."

"Yeah. That's why I didn't know what to say."

"So what did you say?"

"Nothing."

"Nothing?" Ethan's got this look of stunned horror on his face.

"I should have said something, huh?"

Ethan shakes his head in disbelief. "So what happened? I just don't get how this panned out at all. You freaked out and stopped, then gave her no explanation?"

Jon shrugs. "I couldn't think of anything."

"Then you should have told her the fucking truth! Maybe she would have understood. I mean it's a pretty bloody heavy thing to have your mum die. And it was only eight months ago."

They're silent for a minute. It's a long minute.

Ethan breaks the silence. "Does that happen to you much? Y'know. Flashbacks."

"A bit," says Jon. "How about you?"

"I wish I hadn't seen her after she died. Sometimes I can't get it out of my mind."

"They told me it'd be better if you did. Sometimes kids don't really believe it's true."

"I guess," says Ethan.

"I'm just trying to do the right thing. All the time. But I'm only nineteen. Half the time I feel like a little kid myself, but I'm supposed to act like your dad or something."

"I never asked you to."

Jon groans with frustration and anger. "Why do you have to be so fucking immature? At fourteen I was taking care of you and Mum. If you were more like me at fourteen, we wouldn't have a problem." Jon's surprised at the anger in his voice. He's angry at Ethan. Angry at his mother. Angry at his father.

Ethan doesn't know what to say and Jon lets the silence hang a second.

"What do you want to do when we get home? You wanna stay with me? Or get a foster home?" Jon says at last.

"I don't want no shit foster home."

"Then help me, Ethan. If you keep fucking up, it's going to be all over before you know it."

"'Cause I keep getting pissed?"

"Basically."

"It has been getting a bit out of hand."

"More than a bit."

"I think you're sometimes a bit extreme. Because of Mum. I'm not like her, you know. I'm just trying to have fun, break up the boredom, y'know."

But Jon's not giving in. Not this time. "Boredom? What crap. You're on a trip most kids would dream about. You are like her. You use alcohol at every opportunity. It doesn't matter where I take you, you'd be just as happy getting pissed. The only difference I see between you and Sharon is that you're fourteen, not forty-seven. She'd just had longer to stuff up her life and ours. Don't kid yourself. If you're doing this at fourteen, it's only going to get worse unless you decide to change things."

"I'm not going through my whole life not drinking."

"There you go again. For you, having a drink is getting pissed. On your own. And often. For me having a drink is having a beer at the footy or some drinks at the pub when I'm out with friends. You gotta stop kidding yourself. You have a problem."

Ethan looks away.

"And one way or another we have to do something about it when we get home."

"What's going to happen?"

"I don't know."

Ethan has tears welling in his eyes. "You'll put me in a foster home," he mutters through clenched teeth.

Jon wants to put his arm around his brother. But he can't. He softens his voice instead. "I'm hoping we can work this out together. You're all I've got, Ethan."

Ethan glances up at him. "What about your father?" There's a bitter edge to his voice that he's not quite managed to control. It's that odd vague feeling he's been tamping down these past weeks. Jon has a father, and now a sister. Another family that Ethan doesn't belong with. He doesn't know how he feels about that yet. It makes him feel strange. And a little scared.

"Well, we're going home," Jon says evenly. "Now I know where he is, I'll write him a letter."

Ethan shakes his head at this. He's going to be brave. "Don't be stupid. You should go see him," he says.

"How? We're leaving."

"If you go now, you could be back late tomorrow or early the next morning."

"I can't leave you."

Ethan laughs. "Why the fuck not? I'm safe here. I'm stuck in fucking hospital. You could see your father and see Katrin and be back to get the flight to KL day after tomorrow. Come on. I feel like shit stuffing this up. It'd make me feel better."

Jon's looking at him, thinking it over.

"Come on, Jon. Please," says Ethan. "What have you got to lose?"

18

Jon is lying on a mattress. He is naked. There is sweat streaming down his body. His head is pounding.

The walls are brown. They look like logs, but he can see this isn't a log cabin. The logs run vertically. They are just raw timber that's been roughly milled.

The bed is blueish and around the bed there's a row of light blue tiles, stuck to the wall. He hears rushing water. And rain. Always the rain. He feels like he's in a swimming pool.

The sweat that gathers in the skin folds at his neck is uncomfortable. It's making him hotter. He lifts his head. Just a little.

There's no floor here. Jon is confused. Then he realises; this is Katrin's room. The little one.

There's a sharp pain at his thigh. Something is jabbing into him. He lets it. It seems too hard to move. Then he changes his mind and flicks down a hand and it lands on a book. He shifts his head a little and glances down. His Lonely Planet book is there, spread open, face down. A corner presses against him. It hurts. He makes the effort to shove over a little away from the book.

Jon feels like shit. And he'd been reading about why, but it was too confusing. He'd fallen asleep. Now he can't remember what he'd read.

The effort required to pick the book up seems enormous. His neck is aching. He feels sick to his guts. But he's so tired he doesn't think he can get up.

A mosquito circles, noisily. No net. Shit. He'd left it with Ethan. But it's probably too late anyway. His head is swimming. Pain pounding inside his skull in time with his pulse. He swallows, his throat raw, dry, and painful. Then he can't make himself care.

It's dark now. He cannot see a thing. Still there is the sound of rain, heavier than before. And the sound of the river. He is shivering. His body shakes. He has pulled his sleep sheet around himself, but he feels so cold.

What time is it? He gathers himself together. He can't just lie here in the dark. It's too cold. He rolls over painfully. Now he's on his stomach and he's raised himself up to crawling position. Feeling with his hand he makes out the tiled edge of the wall and follows it around.

At the foot of the bed it stops and Jon reaches out for his pack. Tipping it, he finds a T-shirt and puts it on. There's some long pants, but in the dark he can't find boxers. He puts the long pants on. His hands close over his fleece and that goes on as well. It's better, but he still can't control the shaking in his body.

He stumbles to his feet. His hands fumble out in front of him and he makes out the door frame and the switch for the light. He flicks it, but there is no power. He squats beside his pack and rummages through the mess. Eventually his hand closes over the cold, hard steel of his maglite. Flicking it on he makes out the room. The bed is soaked wet, where he was lying, a dark shape where his body has been for several hours. His bowels are aching, but he also wants to chuck. The horrific thought of doing one or both in his room gets him to his feet again. He opens the door.

The river sounds louder. It's totally dark out here, except for the torch light. Jon makes his way along the path towards the bathroom. Thank God it's empty.

This is urgent. Jon feels panicky. He's being overtaken by two involuntary urges at once and can't work out which to give in to first. His bowels win. He has his pants down before he's through the door and he only just gets to a squat and his arse positioned before he loses control.

The feeling is relief and devastation all at once. He starts to vomit, almost losing his footing. His eyes are clamped shut and when he opens them he sees the yellow light from where he dropped his mag. It's lying in a pool of water and vomit, casting a saucer-sized round light in the corner. He feels his insides draining away, but his legs are weak. They wobble and he can barely hold the squat. He puts his hand out and holds the wall. But he's slipping and suddenly he's fallen and his arse and hand are actually in the squat toilet with his mess.

And then he's chucking again. He gets himself up and has enough control to direct the heaves in the direction of the bowl. His skin is burning.

With the cleaner of his two hands he grabs the ladle in the bak mandi and douses the toilet and the floor and then himself. He pours the water right over his head and his clothes. Maybe ten ladles worth. Then his stomach cramps again and he is doubled with pain. His bowels are aching again and he gets himself back over the toilet.

On it goes. He's not sure how long.

Sometime later he's sitting outside the bathroom, too scared to go far away. He's on the ground. His back is against the wall of the building, his legs bent up to his chest. He's wrapped his arms around them and most of the time he rests his head on his knees. He's unbelievably tired and his head is still aching.

A little further away he can dimly make out the glow of oil lamps coming from the Jungle Inn. It can't be that late if it's still open.

He tosses up the idea of going for help. But he can't walk in there looking – and smelling – like this. He's doused himself in water over and again, but the smell on him and in the kamar kecil is disgusting. He knows he'll never get rid of it. Not in the short term. It was like that with Sharon, right before she went to the hospice. No matter what he did, her room always stunk.

His mind is dulled, but still ticking over. Though he can barely raise the energy to move in and out of the bathroom, he knows he's in trouble.

At the very least I'll need water, he thinks, there's none in the room. But he can't see himself making it back there again either.

He's stuck, at least for now.

The French guy's name is Martin. Another Martin. Must be popular in Europe, Jon thinks.

He's nice, though. Jon's still sitting outside the toilet when Martin comes by to use it. First he goes and gets Jon some water and, while Jon's trying to drink it, he goes back to Jon's room, which Jon has left unlocked and he goes through Jon's pack and finds him a change of clothes and his toiletry bag. And he doesn't steal Jon's stuff, which Jon's left lying in his security wallet on the floor. Instead he gathers it up and clips it around his own waist under his shirt, telling Jon not to worry, that he has his stuff and it's safe.

Then, to Jon's shame, Martin undresses him. Gets his wet gear off so that Jon's standing naked – not that there's anyone around to see him. Then Martin holds the door of the mandi open while Jon soaps up and bathes. He washes his hair and brushes his teeth. And when he has to stop to use his bowels and he's saying "I'm sorry" and almost in tears from the shame, Martin just turns his head and says "Don't worry about it."

Then Jon's fairly clean, at least. Though he still feels dreadful. He's able to walk to his room and he falls into bed.

"I will be back," says Martin, but Jon doesn't care one way or the other. His head is pounding again, but he's so tired he thinks he will sleep despite it.

Then Martin is back. He has brought some blankets he has found, which is good because Jon is shivering madly again. Martin packs them around Jon's body, then sits down on the edge of the mattress. "So you eat something?" he asks.

"Not sure," says Jon. It's an effort to speak.

"Have you read in the Lonely Planet?"

"I tried," said Jon. "But everything sounds the same. Maybe it's malaria?"

"Let's see." Martin starts to flick through the health pages. "I see you have no net. You really should have a net here."

"I did," said Jon, but he's too tired to explain. He knows he got bitten a few times when he was trekking, even though they had a net. There were thousands of the things and he wasn't under the net the whole time.

Jon knows about malaria, so he knows Martin skips reading aloud the bit about it being serious and potentially fatal. "Says the symptoms are fever, chills, sweating, headache, diarrhoea… Well, we know you have that…and abdominal cramps." He stops speaking as he reads on. "You have headache? Yes?"

"Yes," agrees Jon.

Martin is still reading. "Maybe also it is dengue fever. You get that from the mosquito also." He reads aloud, "High fever, headache, joint and muscle pain – it used to be called break bone fever – nausea and vomiting. Also a rash, but not for a few days. Sounds the same as malaria."

Jon knows this too. Now he remembers reading this section when he first started feeling like crap this afternoon. It was very confusing. And a bit scary. Dengue, like malaria, can also be fatal, but that's uncommon. There's no treatment: you just suffer through it. Martin is quiet as he absorbs what he reads. Jon suspects he is also reading the bit on Japanese B encephalitis which also has fever and headache as symptoms and is often fatal or causes brain damage. It says it's very rare, though, and Martin doesn't mention it.

"Ah, also there is typhus. It has fever headache and chills. You can get it from ticks that bite – often on the trek. You have done the trek? No?"

"No," says Jon agreeing. "I mean, yes. Yes, I did the trek. Don't know about ticks. Typhus? Is that the same as typhoid?" Jon knows he read this, but he can't remember.

"I don't know."

Jon hears pages flicking.

"No, typhoid is – wait a minute, I must read…typhoid…it is a stomach problem from food or water. There is fever, high temperature, vomiting, diarrhoea… Sounds the same." There's another pause as Martin reads.

"Look also at hepatitis," suggests Jon.

"Fever, chills, weakness, aches and pains…nausea, vomiting…" Martin reads. There is a pause while he takes in some other possibilities: "It could also be dysentery," he says at last. "You get fever and weakness there too. Along with the stomach problems."

"This isn't much help, is it?"

"Not really. I guess that's why there are doctors still and not just the Lonely Planet."

"What time is it?" says Jon.

"About eight-thirty."

"It's earlier than I thought."

"You should sleep. Tomorrow you must go to Medan and visit the hospital."

Sharon is with him. He smells her cigarette breath. He hears the little kissing noise her lips make as they suck in a puff of smoke. It makes him feel safe. Her warm body presses down on the bed beside him as she sits, incenting the mattress. He slides down the incline, nestled against her hip, wanting to be there although he feels desperately hot. She takes a cold cloth and mops his forehead.

"My head hurts," he says, his voice a little whisper. A little boy's whisper.

He opens his eyes. He's in her big bed. He recognises the blue light from the street lamp. She leans over him, her long hair falling down around her face, a line of freckles across her nose. She looks away briefly to put the cigarette aside, then she is back to him. She takes her thumbs and places them on the bridge over his nose. He closes his eyes, knowing this. She starts gently. Little circles, rubbing, massaging outwards, across his forehead, around his temples, onto his cheeks. The pain is released, soothed away. He opens his eyes when she stops.

She smiles at him and leans down and kisses his nose. "Don't worry, sweetie," she says "Mummy's here."

Jon wakes in total darkness, unsure where he is for the third time that day. His clothes are wet with sweat again. He reaches out and his hand bangs painfully against a hard sharp surface. Feeling about he makes out what he thinks are tiles. Katrin's little room. Oh no, he remembers.

After a bit more fishing around he finds his maglite and switches it on. Martin has put his watch close by and some water and he takes a drink and checks the time. It's only nine-thirty p.m. God, this will be a long night, he thinks.

The painkillers he took earlier seem to be working and his stomach has settled a little. Just enough to allow him to worry about other things. Like not wanting to meet his father in this condition. Like Katrin and his own embarrassment. God, he didn't want to go back to Medan and miss his father, but he didn't want to be stuck here either.

He had arrived at Bukit Lawang just after lunch and enquiries soon showed him that Katrin had left that day on a jungle trek.

She's been with her three friends.

He hadn't been nosy, but it hadn't been hard to find out that she spent last night in the upstairs room he'd shared with Ethan, and that her "boyfriend" had been there with her. He'd just asked if she'd had the little room and the information had been volunteered.

He's tried telling himself that maybe Katrin and Martin were just sharing. But he doesn't really believe it. She's never asked to share with him and Ethan. Well except for that one time...

He switches out the light.

Jon is awakened by voices. There's a sharp cry – he can't make out the word. Then the noises are overtaken by a roar. It's distant, in the jungle.

Suddenly he's certain that something dreadful is about to happen. He springs to his feet, standing on the mattress. It's only for an instant. He has time to take one breath and realise there's nothing he can do. That second seems to hang. The roar is all around him.

Then there's a deafening crash as he feels the log wall come at him, picking him up and smashing him flat against the other wall. The impact is enormous and the effect on his body shattering. He's meat in the sandwich. Then he's tumbling over and again between the two walls. He's being wrenched and rotated and flipped and bashed. Everything is black and there's pain all around. He's face up. Then down. His arm wrenched unnaturally backward. He's upside down. Now he's in water.

Now tossed out. The noise is a steady crashing roar interrupted by the dull deadening of sound as his ears are covered by water, uncovered and covered again.

Then, as soon as it started, it is over. He is utterly still, lying face down in water, a heavy weight on his legs, pinning him. He's going to drown.

The thought grips him and in panic he tries to struggle, but he cannot move. He's craning his neck trying to lift his head, like a helpless baby. He tries and tries, though it's hopeless. Then just as he realises he's going to die, the water level suddenly drops and he can breathe again. He gasps once. Twice. He feels some hope, but it's pitch black and he can't move. He's in terrible pain. His body begins to shake. He has no idea what has happened. And then the water washes over him again. This time he's going to die.

18

Gunung Leussuer National Park

Katrin will be glad when this is over. She likes – even loves – the jungle and she's never been shy of physical activity. But the conditions for the past two days have been dreadful.

It isn't just that she's been wet through for nearly forty-eight hours. Though, when you think of it, that is an incredibly long time to have your skin covered in wet cloth.

She's worried about her feet. They are swollen and painful – she's actually been too scared to take her boots off for the past day, for fear she won't be able to get them back on. Or that the skin will fall off.

It's also the leeches. The first day she tried to get them off every time the group stopped walking. She had a bag of salt, but it was all gone pretty quick. Since then she's tried burning them with Jean's cigarettes and pulling them off. Now finally she's ignoring them. They have their fill of her blood and drop off. She doesn't like to think of them under her trousers, but they are there, sucking her blood. They start of the size of a flea, then suck her blood till they're the size of her MP3 player.

She's so tired she can't think straight. Her head feels fuzzy and numb.

Hamid keeps reassuring them they're nearly back, but she's so exhausted that this path looks like all the other paths. They could be anywhere. She hopes to God he knows what he's doing. They'd been so miserable that they'd set off at first light this morning, around six. No one had slept a wink and they were just wanting to be back. They've been slogging it out for an hour and a half now.

Then she comes around a bend and sees something strange. For a second she thinks she's stumbled into the loggers' camp. There's logs and bits of timber everywhere. And churned-up dirt and soil.

Hamid is just behind her. She turns to see him stop dead and drop to his knees. Then he starts to moan. All of a sudden she realises he's praying to Allah.

Suddenly the picture clears for her. Like a pixellated image forming, she places together the familiar and the incomprehensible. Up on the hillside there are a few buildings she recognises. There's the river. There's the orang-utan research station. That even looks like the Jungle Inn. But everything else is just gone. There's no sign of the Bohorok Guest House where they'd been staying. Everything is utterly demolished. Dozens of buildings along the riverbank have just disappeared.

What on earth has happened here?

19

Rumah Sakit Gleneagles, Medan

Ethan wakes to a hand clamped over his mouth. The hospital room is darkened, but Silvan's shock of dyed white hair catches the yellowish light from the hall way. Even in the half light Ethan can see those cold blue eyes boring into him. There's something sharp at his throat. He feels the point biting into his skin and he knows it's the razor.

"So much for fucking Aussie loyalty," hisses Silvan…

He's whimpering aloud as his eyes open and begin to focus on the room. His heart is pounding in the most complete terror. Slowly a sense of relief washes over him. But he can't quite trust it. What just happened was a dream. But something is still wrong.

Down the corridor there's a commotion. People are talking excitedly in Indonesian. In another ward, a woman is wailing loudly, as if in agony.

He keeps hearing the word "*banjir*", which somehow he knows means flood.

It takes him time to get himself out of bed. Everything hurts. His ribs, his ankle. Muscles he didn't know he'd damaged. But he's been given crutches to get to the toilet by himself and he sets off to find out what's going on.

He hobbles up to a cluster of nurses who are talking in an animated fashion. "*Maaf,*" he says. "Excuse me." He wants to ask "What's wrong?" but he doesn't know how to so he just says "*Apa? Apa?* What? What?"

One nurse turns to him and speaks in Indonesian. He catches only the two words "*banjir*" and "Bohorok".

Bohorok? He has a dreadful sinking feeling in his gut.

"Bukit Lawang OK?" he asks.

A different nurse answers, "Bohorok. Bukit Lawang – *sama, sama.* Bad. All gone."

Three hours later, Ethan's on the longest bus ride of his life. How do you pass the time when you think your brother might be dead? You just sit there and stare out the window and try not to think.

But then there's nothing to do but think.

Something wet hits him in the face. He is inside because he's just too banged up to be climbing on the roof. Koko's up there, though. He's come with Ethan because Ethan needs help to do just about anything, especially walk. It's taken him forever to get this organised. He'd begged and begged to be given internet access, but there was no email from Jon. Plus everything he saw on the net just made the situation seem more hopeless. They were talking hundreds, possibly thousands dead. The whole of the tourist settlement was wiped out, plus two villages downstream.

He'd found a doctor to splint his ankle more securely, so he could travel. He'd had to get word to Koko. He'd written a note and had a becak man cycle over to where Koko was staying. They'd borrowed some money using Ethan's camera as security – Jon had only left him the equivalent of about five dollars because you don't need money in hospital. And Jon had the ATM card.

Now he's on a bus heading in the direction of Bukit Lawang.

He's got a window seat. It's one of those old buses that you can slide the windows open, so he's done that. He's kind of jammed in next to this old woman and he's been resting his head on the window sill. His eyes are shut and he's pretending that he's going to try and sleep, but really he's just not in the mood for everyone laughing and pointing and being friendly to him.

Inside his head he's feeling like he's going to scream. Don't you know that the only person I've got in the world might be dead? I might be in this fucking foreign country alone, with no money and no friends? I don't even have my ticket or insurance details. I wouldn't even know what company Jon's put us with. And I'm scared.

A couple of times he's started to panic. His breath has started coming real fast and he's been able to hear himself starting to groan aloud.

I don't know how I'm ever going to live without Jon. This is worse than Mum. When Mum died I had time to get used to it. And I had Jon.

Then something else wet hits him. He opens his eyes.

Rain?

Well, it's more cloudy here. He looks down at the road. The bus is moving pretty slowly because it's in some winding hill country. The road looks dry. There's no rain about, for a change.

Then he looks up along the windows of the bus and more wet hits him.

And then he sees her. That woman vomiting out the window.

The wet stream of spew splatters down the windows of the bus and whooshes in his open one.

He feels the gag coming. He tries to hold it in, then he heaves and the pain explodes in his chest as his cracked ribs complain. He groans aloud then sucks in breath. The old woman sitting next to him pinches his arm so it hurts.

"What?" he says irritably.

She's pointing to the window and making frantic motions for him to slide it shut.

He does so, without looking at her.

The bus is stopped short of Bukit Lawang by a road block. There are people about on motorcycles and Koko arranges one for Ethan.

"Not enough money for both of us," Koko says. "If Jon is not there, we'll be stuck."

"I know. I've got your email address. I'll email you when I can."

Koko shakes Ethan's hand. Ethan thinks Koko's a pretty good guy. Jon had told Koko they'd get him a new bike. He'd taken their word and now was saying goodbye not knowing whether he'd ever see Ethan again.

"*Hati-Hati*, Ethan," he says, his eyes full of genuine concern. "I pray Jon is OK."

"Me too, mate. Me too. Thanks. For everything. I'll email you soon."

Koko speaks to the motorcycle taxi man and he takes off gently so

Ethan can find his balance, holding his busted ankle away from the ground. There's a bar at the back of the seat for him to grasp and he carries his crutches – which he borrowed at the hospital – in his other hand.

The road is a mess. There's four-wheel drives churning it up and soon the motorcycle is making very poor progress, slipping and sliding about. Ethan's nearly fallen off several times and not being able to put his right leg down on the ground is a major handicap when riding pillion on a bike in these conditions.

Eventually he pitches off the right side, protecting his ankle and hitting the mud face-first.

He picks himself up and pays off the motorcycle man. There's no way they can go on.

Looking at the four-wheel drives, he knows he needs to get inside one. But who's going to have him in their car all covered in mud and with almost no money left to pay?

There are people everywhere, but none of them know him. He's completely overwhelmed – tired, distressed. He sits down in the dirt and puts his hands in his face. A lorry roars past him throwing up a spray of muddy water.

And then he's sobbing like he will never be able to stop.

20

Bukit Lawang

She's been at it for two hours now. Clambering over tree trunks and piles of splintered building materials and through knee-deep mud, looking for survivors, helping to free bodies. It's awful. Indescribably awful. She helped drag a dead boy of ten from the mud. How she keeps going, she doesn't know. But she does keep going. All these poor people. And Martin is here somewhere.

God knows where…

He'd chosen not to do the trek. His knee was sore. He'd talked of moving out of the upstairs room while she was gone, to save money. If he'd gone over to the Jungle Inn he might still be alive. But if he took something downstairs…well, the Bohorok Guest House is gone. It doesn't exist any more.

As the morning passes, more and more people arrive. There's wailing villagers looking for family. Fathers looking for sons who were working at Bukit Lawang. Women crying for their children who surely were lost. There's also people from the research station who were above the flood line. They seem to be coordinating things. Then there's police and soldiers and more men in uniform arriving all the time.

There's whispers already about what has caused this. People are saying it was the loggers, that a dam they built up river has burst. There's tree trunks everywhere. Maybe it's true.

Katrin has worked all day, helping search for survivors. A couple of tourists were found up in trees. They'd been walking to their hotel when they heard the roar and instinct sent them to higher ground. Some locals were found half drowned by mud, but still alive. These were miracles, though. There were whispers of hundreds dead. Thousands even.

There are bodies too, though not as many as you'd expect. She's heard many were collected downstream. The ones they found were wrapped in tarpaulins the army brought in.

Now it's dark and Katrin is beyond exhaustion. She's worked all day, because she can't see how you can walk away from this. So she kept going. She's sure there are people alive here, still. And Martin is here somewhere.

Kind, gentle Martin. Looking at the wreck that was where they were staying, she finds it difficult to hold out hope.

Officials have started making lists of the dead and the missing. Each time she takes a break she scans the list of the dead. Now, at the end of the day there are a few dozen names. It doesn't mean a lot. There are many more bodies than names. They just haven't been identified yet. The list of the missing has hundreds of names on it and it's growing all the time. She's already written down Martin's name with the missing.

Sometime that day she managed to get across the message that she has a little medical knowledge. So she'd been pulled off the search and put to work doing basic first aid, cleaning, taping, bandaging. Some emergency medical supplies were being brought in, as well as some doctors and nurses. She's mainly cleaning and bandaging wounds, to try and stop them getting infected. It's awful, but most of the wounded are rescuers, who've cut themselves on corrugated iron, splintered wood and nails.

Now she's going to sleep for a while. Since early this morning she's been separated from her friends. They'd joined the rescue work, but maybe they've been evacuated now, she doesn't know. See hasn't seen them for hours.

Someone has given her a blanket and she's going to find a dry corner in this makeshift hospital. But first she checks the lists. Just one last time for tonight. She doesn't bother with the list of missing. She goes straight to the dead.

And there it is. She feels a pain in her chest.

Martin. Oh, no. Poor Martin. But she had been waiting for it. When the guest house was gone and he was missing, she knew he was dead.

But what she sees next stuns her beyond belief. Next to Martin – Jon's name. Jonathan Subawa.

Katrin feels on the edge of panic. How can it be? Jon is at Lake Toba with Ethan. It must be a mistake. But there's no one around now who can help her clarify how Jon's name got on a list of the dead. Perhaps they're using an old hotel register, she thinks.

But why would they do that? It doesn't make sense.

Perhaps it is his Indonesian surname. Maybe there is someone else called Jonathan Subawa. That must be it. The thought gives her hope. And exhaustion does the rest. "Poor Martin," she says to herself again. Then she falls asleep.

21

Sujiman family home, three kilometres from Bukit Lawang

Ethan's trying to eat. In front of him on a bamboo mat is a plate of boiled rice. There's also some stewed green vegetable and a meat curry. *Kambing.* Goat.

The old man sits cross-legged facing him, his wife next to him. They are eating skilfully with their right hands. They take a small amount of rice between their thumbs and forefingers, add a little meat or vegetable and pop it deftly into their mouths. There are two small children, one between him and the old man and the other between him and the woman. They're a boy and a girl. Ethan can't tell how old. But they're young – maybe five or six. He's impressed with how good they are. No screaming, yelling or fighting. They eat their breakfast hungrily, sneaking curious looks at their strange guest.

The old man had found him by the side of the road last night and brought him home. He showed him a corner he could sleep in and gave him a blanket. He's given him some water and shown him the kettle so Ethan would know it's cooled boiled water, and safe.

They can't communicate much. The old man speaks Indonesian, but not English. Ethan understands that they are the grandparents of the children.

"*Ibu dan bapaknya tinggal di Bukit Lawang.* Their mother and father live at Bukit Lawang," he'd said gravely. Then he'd said something else – Ethan only picked up the one word "*meninggal,* dead". The old man thinks the children's parents are dead. They're probably living away from their family, working the tourist trade.

What will become of these people now? Ethan looks around. This is a two-room shack. It has a dirt floor covered in straw mats. The kitchen is a wood fire in a shed off the side of the house. The toilet is a hole down the back garden. There is no electricity or running water. Things are tough enough now. How will these people survive losing their two young breadwinners?

Ethan lay awake most of the night. He felt grateful to these people and terribly ashamed. He was glad they didn't know him very well. He'd hate them to know how he'd been living his life in their country these past few weeks. A single bottle of beer would feed this family for a whole day.

And now he's feeling dumb buying Koko all that beer, when Koko doesn't even have a job, and then he goes and wrecks his bike.

And those people on the motor scooter. He'd broken that kid's arm. What are they thinking now? Are they worried he'll run off back to Australia without paying for their bike or medical bills?

What a mess he's been making of everything. He looks around and knows he's had opportunities these people could barely imagine. But he thought he was hard done by because his mum died and he didn't have a dad. He thought he was being cool throwing it in Jon's face and pissing it all up against the wall.

And now Jon might be dead.

He'd cried in this old man's arms last night. Sobbed his heart out against his bony chest, wetting his shirt with his tears.

Afterwards he'd tried to explain. "*Kakak laki-laki saya.* Bukit Lawang. My older brother. Bukit Lawang."

"*Meninggal?*" said the old man.

Ethan had shrugged, because he couldn't trust himself to speak. Then swallowing down a sob he'd said, "Maybe,' then, "I think so."

By nine a.m. he's in the back of an army lorry full of troops. It cost him his last two ten thousand notes to bribe his way on board. That left him with five thousand for the old man. Less than a dollar for two meals, a night's accommodation and his help this morning striking a deal with these soldiers. The old man seemed happy enough and waved goodbye like this kind of thing happened to him all the time.

As he watched him, Ethan wondered whether Australians would be so generous as to take a foreigner into their house to sleep in the same bedroom with their children for the night. And especially now, with their own fears for their family. Yet they'd been so kind to him.

It isn't far. About ten minutes later they're pulling up. A couple of powerful-looking soldiers lift Ethan down from the lorry and hand him his crutches.

Then he sees Katrin. And she sees him.

At that moment, he knows all is lost. It's the look of anguish on her face when she realises it's him.

When Katrin sees Ethan she knows for absolute sure that no mistake has been made. There can only be one reason why Ethan would arrive here alone. Jon must have been here.

It is devastating. Since first light she's been wandering around trying to find the right people to talk to about her friends.

It isn't easy. There's a list that says both men are dead, but she has taken some time to find out where their bodies have supposedly been taken.

The moment she undid the tarpaulin and saw Martin was the worst of her life.

Jon has been more difficult to locate. His body wasn't with Martin's, but then maybe he'd been taken out to the hospital. Or maybe his body is at a mortuary downstream.

But his passport is here. Sopping wet in his pouch, it is now in a plastic bag with Martin's passport and some others belonging to foreigners.

"Where is he?" Katrin can't bear to look at the grief on Ethan's face.

"Ethan..." she whispers, "are you sure?" After seeing Martin, she doesn't want him to go through that with his own brother.

"I want to see him."

They're sitting together in the back seat of a four-wheel drive waiting to be evacuated. They'll be taken first to a local hospital at Biniai, which is somewhere back towards Medan. After that? It's too hard to think about.

Ethan is in shock. He's said little, but several times has repeated that he wants to see his brother.

Biniai hospital is crowded and finding it hard to cope with the injured. They're lying on stretchers, the floor, sitting on blankets and stools. There are at least a hundred people waiting for medical attention, as well as family and friends. She's seen bones broken, dislocations, dreadful lacerations.

Katrin can't see the point in hanging around. The flood wiped out the tourist resort at Bukit Lawang – about thirty or forty hotels, though most were empty apart from staff. Then it charged through the villages down river. Word is that there are several hundred dead and injured locals and about 1,500 homeless people – at least four hundred houses just don't exist any more. The best thing she and Ethan can do is get out of the way and free up resources.

But Jon might be here. Katrin can't just leave without knowing, so she goes looking for lists. Maybe there's a mortuary list.

It is chaotic. Everyone is incredibly busy. It's brush off after brush off. But Binai Hospital isn't a big place, so she starts going from room to room, corridor by corridor. She can't leave Ethan by himself, so he hobbles along behind her as if in a daze.

She walks straight into a ward, goes up to the nurse and says. "*Teman saya di rumah sakit. Namanya Jonathan Subawa. Di mana?*" It's pretty basic Indonesian: "My friend is in the hospital. His name is Jonathan Subawa. Where is he?" Then she tries another ward, then another and another.

Mostly she's waved away. Sometimes people show her a list, which she scans. She doesn't know how to say "dead" and she doesn't want to ask Ethan.

Once when he's standing a bit further off and looking in the other direction she says, "*Teman saya…*" then she feigns being dead with her face. She feels disrespectful doing it and the nurse looks at her in disbelief. From then on she leaves out the theatrics. She keeps asking everyone she meets and figures eventually they'll stumble onto the mortuary.

Then someone looks at her list and says, "*Di sini.*" She's a young woman in a nurse's uniform, wearing the hijab. She smiles. "*Jonathan Subawa di sana. Di sana.*" She's pointing.

It's a crowded ward with a central corridor and about thirty beds running down either side. And it's not full of dead people.

Katrin doesn't walk, she runs. It's easy to see which patients aren't Jon. There's old men and boys, with all manner of injuries and sicknesses that have nothing to do with the flood. She's three quarters down the room when she sees a familiar half-face. The other half is covered in a clean white dressing.

"Jon!" she screams. She had the worst moment of her life this morning, finding Martin. This is possibly the best.

The one eye opens briefly and there's a satisfied glint of recognition. "Katrin," Jon mutters. "Where's Ethan?"

"He's here. He's safe," she says.

Ethan's finally got there, powering along on his crutches. "Bloody hell!" Ethan gasps, a bit short of breath. "They told me you were dead. We're looking for your fucking body here, man."

"Well, you found it. But I'm still here."

"Are you badly hurt?" asks Katrin.

"Kind of. A dislocated shoulder. Lots of cuts. Broken bones in my face. They think I have dengue fever."

"But you're going to be OK?" asks Ethan.

"Yeah. But I still don't know how. I remember drowning, then waking up here."

"Your document pouch…" Katrin is thinking aloud. "I saw it. They said it was found on your body."

Jon looks puzzled. Then he remembers. "There was a guy. He had it. He was helping me."

"Martin," says Katrin.

"That was your friend Martin?"

"Yes. It must have been. He's dead."

"Oh no," says Jon. "He was nice. He helped me."

"His parents…" Katrin trails off. She has to stop speaking, or the tears will come.

Martin had carried a photograph of his parents – he'd been proud of them and very emotional when he told her how supportive they had been when he finally told them he was gay. Now they will be told he is dead.

Jon puts his hand on hers. "I'm so sorry, Katrin," he says.

"It's awful," she says finally. "So many dead…"

"What about your father?" asks Ethan.

Katrin flashes him an annoyed warning look. Now's not the time to worry Jon that his long-lost father might be dead, she's saying with her eyes.

But Jon's face brightens. "Funny you mention it… He just came by. He saw my name on the ward list and came out of curiosity. Another Subawa he didn't know. It was a surprise, to say the least, to find me."

"Bloody hell," says Ethan.

"When?" asks Katrin.

"Just before… Not sure how long. Maybe an hour?"

"How fucking weird is that?" says Ethan.

"Pretty weird," laughs Jon. "And my sister…" Jon has to stop to cough. It's painful to him and he winces.

"Dead?" says Ethan.

"No. She's here. In a ward with the women. My father's house was set back from the river and they're all OK. My sister fell and broke her arm in the debris this morning. I haven't met her yet…" He trails off.

There's a dreaminess in the tone of his voice and Katrin suspects he's been given morphine. She sees strapping to a shoulder and there's a lot of bandages around both legs.

"What's your dad like?" asks Ethan.

"Nice. I guess." It's a weak description. How do you describe meeting your father, for the first time since you were five? Then Jon's one eye sparks up and he smiles as he sees someone standing behind Ethan. "This is him now. You can see for yourself."

Ethan turns to see a man standing watching them. The hairs on the back of his neck prickle.

Darwin Subawa is younger than Ethan ever imagined, and fit and strong – so much so that he almost seems closer to Jon's age than Sharon's. He is smiling, his face warm and friendly.

"*Bapak,*" says Jon. "*Kenalkan. Ini adik saya, Ethan dan teman saya Katrin.* Father, this is my brother Ethan and my friend Katrin.'

"Hello, Katrin," says Darwin Subawa, extending his hand. "Pleased to meet you." His English is excellent.

"Pleased to meet you, *Pak*," says Katrin.

"And Ethan," he says taking Ethan's hand. "You look so much like your mother."

Ethan blushes. For once he's lost for words, so he echoes Katrin and says, "Pleased to meet you, *Pak.*"

Darwin Subawa moves close to Jon and Jon asks about Ani, Darwin's daughter.

"She is fine," Darwin says. "Her mother is with her. This afternoon we will all go back home."

Katrin joins in the conversation, but Ethan is happy to watch and listen as they chat, his eyes darting backwards and forwards between Jon and his father. The similarity is uncanny. He's lanky, like Jon, with that wiry muscular build, but he's not as tall. His skin is a little darker, his nose a little wider, his hair straighter and flecked with grey. His eyes are also darker than Jon's – they're such a dark brown, they're almost black – but they have that same patient kindness behind them. He's like a condensed, more exaggerated version of Jon.

But as Ethan watches, something funny starts to happen. It's weird, almost like eyes adjusting to a change in light. Looking at father and son, side by side, he starts to see traces of Sharon in Jon's face. It was always Ethan that looked like his mother – light brown hair, green eyes, pale skin with a few freckles. Jon had never looked much like either of them, with his brown skin, dark hair and Asian looks. But there she is. Her nose – not Darwin's. The shape of her mouth. It's hard to believe he's never seen it before. Ethan feels a tightness in his throat and tears behind his eyes. He swallows and holds them back.

Soon Darwin is leaving. "I must collect Ani and Sulustri, my wife," he says. "When will I see you again?"

"I'm not sure," says Jon. "We have to go back to Australia as soon as possible so Ethan can get his foot fixed. But first we must get a new passport from the Australian consulate."

"But you will be here tomorrow morning?"

"Yes."

"Then I shall come then. Maybe I can help you with your transportation. Plus I shall bring Ani to meet you. Today is very difficult for her as she is hurt and we have many friends who have been killed. But tonight I will explain to her that she has a brother. That is a good thing, in all this bad. She will be happy about that at least."

"That'd be great," says Jon.

Ethan can see he's relieved he doesn't have to say a proper goodbye now. It's just a little goodbye, until tomorrow.

As Darwin leaves, he puts a hand on Jon's good arm and gives him a squeeze. "*Sampai nanti*," he says. "See you later."

"*Sampai nanti*," says Jon.

They watch Darwin as he leaves. At the doorway he turns and waves to them. They wave back, all three of them.

Now he's gone, Jon looks exhausted. He reaches his hand out and Ethan takes it. "This is pretty weird stuff," he says, his voice a croaky whisper.

"Nah, it's pretty cool, I reckon," says Ethan.

"The whole thing's a disaster. I've just found my father and sister, but their village just got wiped out. Instead of being here to help, I'm all banged-up and have to go home to Australia."

"At least they're alive," says Katrin. "And at least you've found them. That is a miracle, I think."

"Yeah and you'll be able to help them out from back home," says Ethan.

"But I can't even see how to get home. Your passport's lost. Mine's ruined. God knows where the tickets are."

Ethan gives Jon's hand a squeeze. "Don't stress, Jon," he says. "Everything's cool. Tomorrow we'll sort it all out, Katrin and I. My dumb-assed bike accident might cost us a bomb, but this flood mess is definitely covered by insurance."

Jon narrows his eye at Ethan. He isn't convinced.

Ethan gives his hand another squeeze. "Come on, Jon – trust me!" he says.

22

His lungs swell and contract rhythmically with each breath he takes. In, out. In, out. In, out. He locks his mind to the pattern and tries to merge into it.

Perspiration mixes with the grit of sand sticking to his chest. It's hot and Ethan's nearing the end of his endurance. His mind starts to protest the physical pain and he searches for distractions.

There are plenty about. This is Kuta beach and there's no shortage of action.

Ahead are three cute girls, lying on beach towels soaking up the sun. They're lying face down, which is unfortunate, because they're topless. It's culturally pretty disrespectful. The Balinese hate this sort of thing, according to the guide books. Ethan slows right down as he runs past, but it isn't his lucky day.

Now he's watching a fat Japanese guy and his skinny girlfriend, walking hand in hand down to the surf. The sun is hot and bright, glistening like flakes of silver on the white caps of the waves. The sky is a deep blue. Rows of waves crash in and there's a nasty undertow that makes the shallow water swirl around. Beyond the break there's packs of guys – and a few girls – Indonesian, Western, Japanese – bobbing up on down on boards, catching rides on the powerful waves. On the shore, muscular Balinese surf lifesavers sit around ready to go. It's a serious business. People drown here all the time.

Ethan's eyes pan back and upwards to take in the icons of Kuta beach. The palm trees that ring the perfect semicircle of white sand. The yellow and red surf rescue flags. Behind that, the roofs of hotels. A mobile phone tower. The golden arches of McDonalds and the most enormous Marlboro cigarette sign towering over everything.

It ain't Sumatra. But it ain't home either. It's got a freaky edge to it, that you just have to go with.

There's always stuff happening on the beach, even though the locals all say there's half the number of tourists there used to be. Bloody terrorists.

The Balinese are really pissed off. It's really hard for them to make a living when there's not enough tourists to go around. A lot of bars and restaurants are empty and the locals are worried. Some are saying it's going to be as bad as the bombings in 2002, but it's only been a couple of weeks since the latest bombs went off. Ethan was still happy to come to Bali. No one stopped going to London or New York, did they?

But for now there's not lot a whole lot the locals can do about it, except try harder. Bored sellers wander hopelessly from person to person. It's nothing anyone really needs. There's rings, watches, cigarettes. There's oil paintings of lime-green waterfalls and peacocks and Polynesian girls half submerged in tropical lagoons – they're truly awful. Surely no one ever buys them. The most luckless sellers are the ones lugging those heavy-looking wood carvings up and down the beach all day long. They've got boxes of chopsticks, wood chimes, puppets, samurai swords, miniature surfboards that say "Bali", bamboo place mats – some one even tried to sell him a giant cuckoo clock. It's pretty odd really.

But then souvenirs are not really his thing. He'd brought nothing back from Sumatra but photographs.

Every three steps some Balinese girl calls "manicure" or "plait your hair". There are women with stacks of pineapples balanced in baskets. They'll drop to the sand, whip out a machete and peel a pineapple for you at the hint of interest. Tattoo artists show off pages from their book of designs. They'll talk you round if you let them then paint you with henna ink on the spot before you've had a chance to think twice.

Everywhere he goes, people call out "Surfboard" and "Transport". He was dozing on his beach towel yesterday when some guy woke him to say, "You want transport?"

"Do I look like I want transport?" he'd grumbled.

"Cigarette lighter?" the guy had said hopefully.

And that's just the legal stuff. All the time he hears young men hissing "Marijuana" or "Ecstasy" as he goes by. Sometimes there's a quietly whispered "You want girl?" When he says no, the cheekier ones break into giggles and call loudly, "You want boy?"

He's tempted to stop and call their bluff. But then again, they probably know someone who'll be up for it and then he'll be stuffed – you don't want to mess with these people.

He loves this feeling, of being away from home, of everything being different and just a little bit dangerous. He doesn't like to think about bombs, but of course it is always there in the back of your mind.

Stepping off the plane three days ago into that thick tropical heat had been a massive buzz. You could smell the difference, even at the airport. The smell of rotting mangoes, clove cigarettes, jet fumes, incense. The wait to get through customs seemed endless. He was dying to get out and have a look around.

The flight was pretty weird. Everyone was really pissed. Well, everyone except him and Marilyn and Dinny. The passengers didn't seem subdued to him. He'd thought they would be, with the bombs and everything. Six hours of free airline booze and a couple of hundred Aussies partying in the aisles. It was like a special kind of torture designed just for him. He'd been in a really shit mood the whole time.

But once they were on the ground and everyone was out of the plane, Ethan was glad to be sober. Glad not to be one of these embarrassing tourists swaying away, unable to stand entirely straight in the queue, talking loudly about crap, and throwing their arms around people they'd just met on the plane.

Ethan likes it here. It's got most of the good things about Sumatra, plus some added bonuses. Like Waterbom Park. And surfing.

Tomorrow he's going to ditch Marilyn. She's taking Dinny off to some famous artist village to look at some paintings and see some dances. To liven it up they're going to see some jewellery making and woodcarving.

It's Ethan's idea of a slow, slow death.

He's going to go paragliding. The day after that he's arranged white water rafting. He's hoping this whole trip can be like this until Jon gets here. Then who knows what will happen. Jon's been living at Darwin's house in his little Sumatran village for months now. Hopefully he'll be sick of culture by now and up for a good time.

Ethan jogs up the stairs of the beach-front palace they've got on this package deal. Who'd go backpacking? Jon must be dumb to stay in those cheap places when you can get a package with airfare that includes something like this. This hotel is the nicest place he's ever seen. It has an enormous blue pool the size of a football field. You can swim up to the bar for a fruit shake. After that you can get pizza in the beach front restaurant – or duck down the road for KFC, Maccas – whatever. And there are girls everywhere. It's totally special.

In the lounge area of their "de luxe suite" Marilyn is rolling on the floor with Dinny. Ethan hears his high-pitched screams of delight and her growls, like a bear, but they're behind the couch and he can just see Maz's legs and bare feet poking out.

Ethan grabs a towel to mop the sweat and guzzles down a litre of water. Tidiness is not Marilyn's strong point and there's plastic bottles scattered everywhere. Tap water in a four-star hotel is still tap water. You don't even brush your teeth with it.

He pokes his head over the couch to see mother and her bub lying spread-eagled next to each other.

All of a sudden she rolls on top of the boy and pulls his T-shirt up and blows the biggest raspberry on his stomach. Dinny just explodes, overcome by the unbearable tickles. His little feet flap madly and he wriggles to be free, breaking away across the floor.

Ethan stands and watches as he towels himself dry. Eventually Marilyn sees him and calls, "Hi, Ethan. Good run? How's the ankle?"

"Not too bad," he says. "Running on the sand is pretty good."

Now he takes over from Marilyn, dropping to the floor and tickling Dinny on his tummy. "Hey there, little man!" he says as Dinny's eyes light up to see him.

Ethan's learned to growl like a bear too and now he's gnawing at Dinny's neck and making the most shameless baby noises. Dinny loves it and again he's squealing.

Marilyn hauls herself up on to the couch. "Found a good map for you," says Marilyn. "It's a really detailed map of Sumatra."

"Cool. Thanks, Maz," he says. Ethan had had this bright idea about making an electronic game about travelling. Kind of a mystery where someone's lost and someone's trying to track them down. Even though he's sort of given up the idea for now, Marilyn keeps saving him stuff. He keeps it all in a plastic bag in his room at home.

His room. His home. He's been living with Marilyn for nearly eighteen months, now. Firstly he and Jon had moved in. Jon met Marilyn at uni – she's a mature-age student and she needed the rent money. And Ethan reckons Marilyn and Jon must have bonded a lot before he even got introduced. It's just too much a coincidence that she's so together on all the drinking stuff. Her way is Alcoholics Anonymous. It isn't Ethan's thing, but she isn't pushy and Ethan really likes living with her. And now Jon's shouting him this cheap package deal to Bali, and Maz says she's got just the excuse to come along too.

When the bombs went off, Ethan was scared she'd pull the plug. But she'd muttered something about lightning not striking twice. It didn't seem a good idea to point out that actually it had just struck twice. And that in Sumatra the Boxing Day Tsunami had come along a year after the flood at Bukit Lawang and killed 200,000 people.

Jon was in Sumatra for the tsunami. For the second year in a row Ethan had endured an anxious wait to find out that he was OK. But Bohorok village was nowhere near the coast, so at least the second time he'd known the chances were remote that Jon was affected. Still, he'd had that same sickening feeling in his gut that he couldn't get away from. Jon'd sent the email saying he was OK on Boxing Day, but the internet was crawling along because of the increase in traffic and the email didn't arrive for two days.

It was funny that of the two of them, it had been Jon who had really struggled to settle down, once they'd gotten home. He'd battled through another semester at uni, then deferred and gotten a job working with an aid agency working on the reconstruction at Bohorok village and Bukit Lawang. It meant he was able to see his father and get to know Ani.

Ethan was lucky Marilyn was around because he was still just fifteen then. He didn't want to go back to Sumatra – he had school, a part-time job, friends – and Marilyn had agreed to foster him.

"I can't just leave you," Jon had said.

"Don't be stupid. Go! I'd come if it bothered me. Don't worry," said Ethan.

"But you'd miss school."

"As if that would stop me! I'm happy here – you're not. So go. And don't think of hanging around here, just to keep an eye on me. I'm fine. I've got Maz to keep me on the straight and narrow."

And she did, too. Fostering Ethan means some extra cash for her, but Ethan knows she really cares for him.

She said to him once, "The day Dinny was born, my life changed. I was thirty-eight years old and a little baby gave me the meaning of life. I'd been missing it the whole time."

"So what is it?"

"What?"

"The meaning!"

"Oh y'know. Mushy stuff teenagers hate."

Ethan groaned, "That'd be right."

"You'll know one day. When you're a dad. Everyone is somebody's baby. After Dinny was born I couldn't watch the news for months. I'd start crying through every story like it had happened to Dinny."

He'd been frowning, thinking for a second of that poor old Sumatran man who had taken him in. Even though he'd found Jon, and everything had worked out for them, that old man really had lost his son. So had lots of other people. He wondered what their lives were like now.

And he'd thought of Koko. And that family he'd run off the road. He'd finally worked enough Friday and Saturday nights at Maccas to pay Jon back for everything he'd had to spend. But the emails and letters he'd sent to Koko and that family were never answered.

He'd been silent a moment too long and Marilyn had misunderstood his mood.

She had come over and put an arm around him, saying "You can be sure that your mother loved you, Ethan." She'd squeezed him hard. "Trust me, OK?"

And he did trust her, so he had let her hold him for a second. Then because he's sixteen, not three, he'd pulled away.

Soon they're on the beach, looking for a spot among the palm trees, keeping to the shade. That sun is blisteringly hot. There are lots of people with red raw skin from being out there too long. They look idiotic, getting that burned.

Right now, Marilyn is spreading towels out. Ethan's grabbed Dinny by his ankles and he's dangling him head down. He's having a good time, but he also scouts around to see if there are any girls watching. He's learned a lot about girls lately. For starters, they're total suckers for a guy who's good with kids. Just look at how Katrin warmed up to Jon as soon as she saw him with Ani. She's flown out twice to see him in her university holidays. He doesn't say much, but Ethan thinks things are going well.

Ethan's proud of Jon and what he's done to help Darwin's village. So much so, that he even helped out a bit, himself. He got his school to raise some money for the village, to rebuild their primary school. That shocked a few people. Once he even gave a short talk in front of assembly. He had pictures from his trip, plus stuff he got off the net. There were several sites that had pictures of the disaster site, before and after. It looked amazing. He'd put it all together in a PowerPoint presentation, then used the data projector to put it all up on the big screen. Kids couldn't believe it when he showed them where Jon had been when the flood hit.

An hour later, Ethan's trying to surf. It shouldn't be that hard. This surfboard he's hired is about twenty feet long. It nearly killed him dragging it down to the water. And now you could float a family of four on it, it's so buoyant.

But those crazy Kuta waves keep picking him up and chucking him down. It's bloody frustrating. And there's Maz laying in the shade under the palm trees watching him. Now he feels like he has to stay and look like he's making progress.

But he's swallowed quite a bit of salt water. It's making him thirsty. He has a bit of a fantasy about sitting down at one of those ramshackle beach bars and ordering an icy-cold Bintang. Kuta beach is very relaxed and chilled out. Traders have set up clusters of plastic chairs around eskies with iced soft drink and beer. When the sun goes down it sets right over the water, like a red ball of flame dousing itself. It's a nice view sober, but a beer would just set it off perfectly.

But he's learned not to dwell on things. And this whole taking a break from booze thing has its benefits.

Ethan looks across at a couple of tall, athletic-looking girls wrestling with a surfboard just like his. He's seen them looking at him.

He's certainly looked the better option on a few occasions now. He's been the cooler one. The one who isn't making a jerk of himself. The one who isn't spewing up or being loud and disgusting. Funnily enough, girls seem to prefer that. It's made the time go easier.

Now the deal is over. He's free to choose.

He'd held up his end of the bargain he made with Jon – not one single alcoholic drink until you're sixteen.

That's Jon – always trying to do the right thing, but not quite nailing it.

Who bans a fourteen-year-old drunk from boozing until he's sixteen? What a dumb idea? That's two years short of the legal age! But Ethan thought he was getting off lightly. He had listened to the plan and kept a straight face because Jon was really, really serious and Ethan knew he'd stuffed up badly. Just the hint of a smirk or a smart comment and he was sure Jon would have had a fit.

They'd been in a hotel room in Medan, waiting for Ethan's replacement passport to arrive by courier from the consulate.

Jon had insisted on another serious chat and Ethan had decided that this time he was going to take it easy on Jon. Jon looked and sounded exhausted. He'd nearly died, after all, and he was still all banged up. It was all pretty stressful and the last thing Jon needed from Ethan at that time was a fight.

So Ethan had taken on the challenge. And now look at him. He prefers this new Ethan. He's fit, muscular. Girls look at him all the time.

So he hadn't rushed out and hit the booze straight away – Maz would've killed him! For his sixteenth, they'd gone out for pizza and they'd drunk a stack of Coke together. It was a good night.

He doesn't know when he'll have his first beer, but he's not really worried about it. Jon always saw drinking as weakness, but Ethan's got a different way of thinking about it. He'd put a lot of effort into getting pissed all the time – like that time when he'd gone out at night and bought the Mansion House whisky. He'd been chasing the thrill, but he'd gone too far.

Recently he's put a lot of effort into staying sober. Even though it has sometimes been really annoying, he's stuck with it.

Now he's got to put an effort into finding a balance. That's all. How hard can it be?

As he approaches Marilyn, he sees she's made some friends already. There's about ten local women clustered around with plastic bags full of plastic jewellery and sarongs. They've recognised Maz from yesterday and word has spread. She'd liked the sarongs and had been trying to choose between two. The first price for one was eighty thousand. So she'd asked, "How much for two?" The woman had said 200,000. Maz had been a bit vacant and had said, "Sure, why not."

Now everyone wants a piece of her.

"You want a Coke?" Ethan says when he gets to her.

"No thanks. I was chatting with an Aussie bloke – his name is Ethan too – he's just gone for some."

"What about Dinny?"

"The bloke said he'd get him something."

"Won't be long," Ethan says. He wanders down the path towards a stall.

There are people everywhere, tourists and locals.

Then, like a dream, he sees this haggard, sun-browned body in cut-off shorts and faded Red Bull T-shirt.

The man's looking sideways, away from Ethan – out towards the ocean. But there's no mistaking that tangled mass of white surfer's hair. Silvan.

He's walking along holding a bottle of Bintang, a Coke and an ice cream. As Silvan passes him, he straightens his gaze to the path, so that Ethan is able to get a good look at those cold blue eyes. They stare right through him. Silvan walks right on by. There's not a glint of recognition.

It isn't surprising. Ethan's nearly six feet tall now. He doesn't look much like the fourteen-year-old boy Silvan met two years ago.

Ethan wheels around to watch what Silvan does next.

To Ethan's utter horror, Silvan walks straight up to where Maz and Dinny are sitting and sits down on their mat, handing Maz the Coke and Dinny the ice cream.

Ethan's heart nearly stops. His mind races. Ethan has this image of pulling away from Silvan, the stretch of his money belt. The sound of it snapping off in the old man's hand.

His name is Ethan too. That cheeky bastard.

Great. What now?

Ethan knows he's been in a situation like this once before and his stuff up that time was monumental.

His mind ticks over quickly, remembering how last time he'd wanted to be a hero but he'd screwed up really badly.

He doesn't want to make a mistake here. That's Marilyn and Dinny over there.

The options slip through his mind quickly. If I go for the cops it might take me twenty minutes to find someone. If I leave Silvan with

Maz and Dinny for twenty minutes, who knows what might happen? Maybe he'll rip them off.

Hell. Maybe he'll take Dinny and sell him – Ethan's heard of that sort of thing. He could just offer to take him to the toilets, or for a swim – then he just disappears… He wouldn't put anything past Silvan.

He can't gamble with this. He's got to handle it himself. This is a public place. What can Silvan do?

Ethan walks over to where Marilyn, Silvan and Dinny are sitting. Standing with the sun behind him, he summons up every bit of man he's got in him. His voice when it comes out is so cold he chills even himself. "Give me back my passport you old prick." He pauses until Silvan's had a chance to take in what's happening.

The next bit he says slowly in a low voice, like he really means it. "Or I'm gunna kick your fucking head right off your shoulders."

Silvan looks startled. He's gazing up into the sun, squinting. Not quite seeing much except for a large shadow of a well built man, his fists clenched at his sides.

"Sorry, matey… I don't believe we've met," Silvan says slowly.

"Ethan!" says Maz, shocked. Instinctively she's drawn Dinny up close to her – not sure what's going on. Obviously she's not seen Ethan like this before.

But it's a big enough clue for Silvan. Ethan sees the glint of recognition – and of fear – in Silvan's eyes.

"Chill, matey, chill. No harm done. Long time no see."

"Hand it over. Now." He's kept his voice level and as menacing as he can get it. He steps forward just a fraction.

"OK! OK! Here!" Silvan pulls a pouch from inside his shirt, whips out a battered-looking Australian passport. He tosses it in Ethan's direction and starts to scramble to his feet.

Ethan lets him get up and start to walk away before he leans down and picks up the passport. He waits until Silvan is out of sight before he takes his eyes off him.

Now he flicks open the front cover. Whoever altered it did a pretty good job. The picture is of Silvan, but it's Ethan's name and his passport number. It's even got his date of birth – 1 October – with 1989 changed to 1949.

Ethan's passport has seen a lot of the world in the past two years. As he turns the pages he sees stamps from a dozen African and Asian countries – he sees Morocco, Kenya, India, Malaysia, Thailand, Vietnam and China at a glance.

Bloody hell, thinks Ethan. I'm probably wanted by the cops in half these countries.

He flicks back to look at his name – Ethan Turner – next to Silvan's picture. It's an especially sinister-looking photo.

Ethan smiles. Now that's a cool souvenir.

Afterword

The events described at Bukit Lawang are based on the real flood that hit the area suddenly on the night of 2 November 2003. It was a tragedy that killed around three hundred people.

I wasn't there for the flood and have based my account of what happened that night and on the days afterwards on the recollections of survivors. I was at Bukit Lawang at the same time of year three years before the flood. My descriptions of the environment, the weather and the accommodation at Bukit Lawang are based on these experiences. I regret any inaccuracies that have resulted due to development and remodelling in the intervening period.